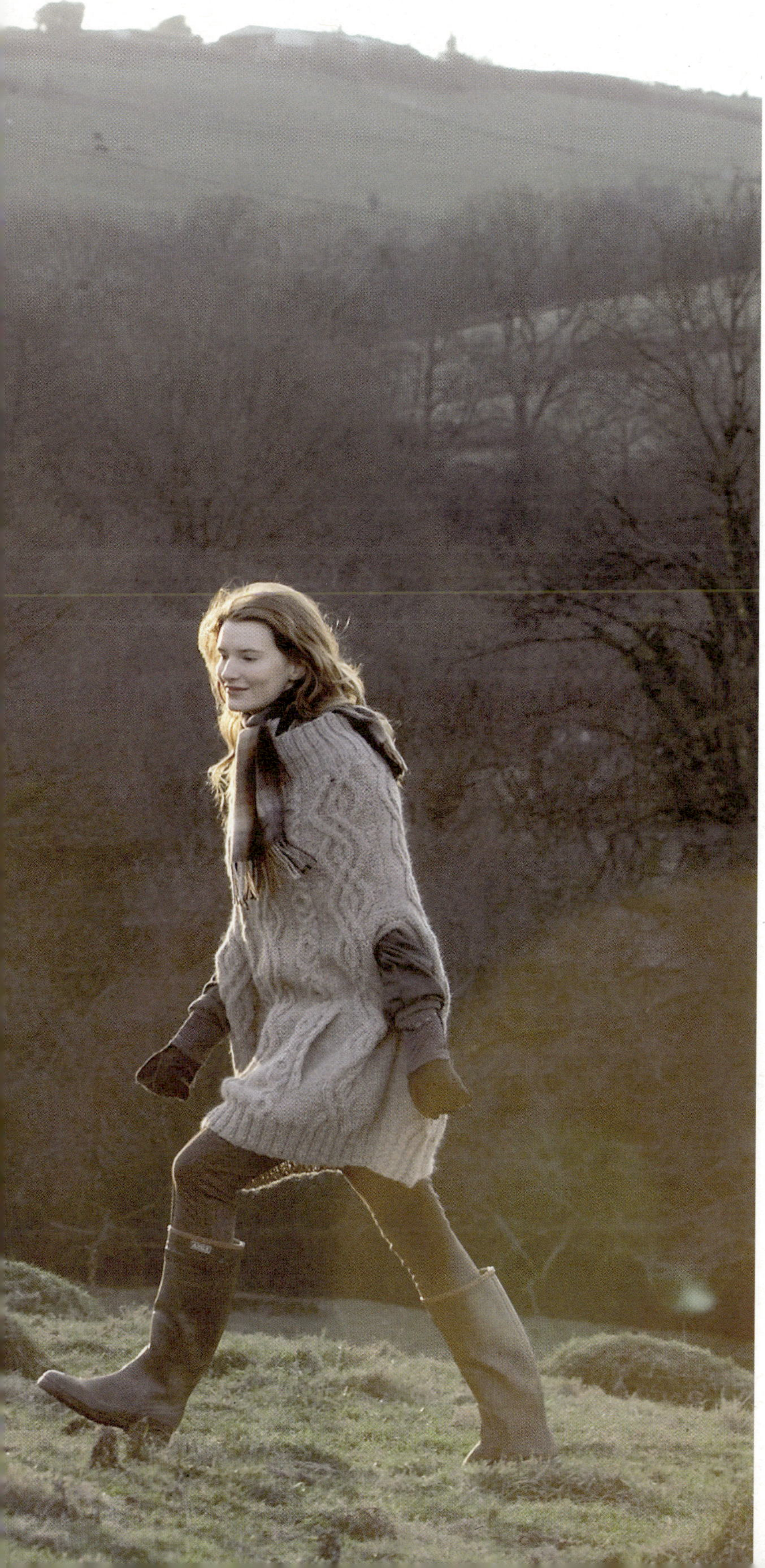

17 designs by Marie Wallin
using Rowan Purelife
Renew, British Sheep Breeds Chunky
& Bouclé

thinkcleanknitgreen

mahonia
british sheep breeds chunky
pattern page 70

winter aconite
renew
pattern page 64

winter aconite
renew
pattern page 64

azara scarf
british sheep breeds chunky
pattern page 52

erica
british sheep breeds chunky
pattern page 56

winter cherry
british sheep breeds chunky
pattern page 67

gorse
british sheep breeds bouclé
pattern page 57

amaryllis
british sheep breeds chunky
pattern page 49

winter sweet
renew
pattern page 74

wild saffron
renew
pattern page 72

wild saffron
renew
pattern page 72

quince
british sheep breeds bouclé
pattern page 60

acacia
british sheep breeds bouclé
pattern page 48

cyclamen
renew
pattern page 54

senna
renew
pattern page 62

snowdrop wrap
renew
pattern page 66

crocus
renew
pattern page 53

crocus
renew
pattern page 53

daphne
renew
pattern page 69

periwinkle
renew
pattern page 59

The British Sheep Breeds

As an annually renewable natural resource, our British wool is shorn and blended from British sheep and spun into beautiful undyed yarn.

Black Welsh

In Wales this sheep is known as 'Cochddu' meaning 'brownish'. This hardy sheep produces fleece which is black, short and thick with a firm handle, durable, light weight and warm.

Shetland Moorit

The Shetland breed of sheep is a small, hardy animal producing fine soft wool. They are farmed on the Shetland Islands but are now more commonly found throughout the UK. Their wool is used exclusively for knitwear, fine shawls and soft woven fabrics.

Jacob

Jacob sheep are generally considered to be an ornamental breed and are often adorned with two, four or even six horns. They are believed to originate from Mesopotamia in Biblical times. The fleece produces naturally blended shades of brown and creamy white.

Suffolk

These sheep are widely spread through out the United Kingdom. The fleece is moderately short with fine fibres.

Bluefaced Leicester

Wool of the Bluefaced Leicester is fairly fine, dense and demi-lustrous, soft to the touch, drapes well and feels comfortable next to the skin.

British Sheep Breeds Bouclé

Since the successful launch of our British Sheep Breeds Chunky & DK yarn , we have been busy working closely with the spinner to develop British Sheep Breeds wool into new exciting yarns. This season sees the launch of our new British Sheep Breeds Bouclé. This beautiful, soft wool lends itself perfectly for designs wonderful for indoor & outdoor wear.

The British Sheep Breeds Bouclé yarn is spun using wool entirely from Bluefaced Leicester sheep and the colour therefore is only available in Ecru.

We hope that you will enjoy knitting and wearing our new British Sheep Breeds Bouclé with the benefit and knowledge that you will be helping our British hill farmers by increasing the demand for British wool and therefore helping to raise the price paid per fleece to the farmer.

As the whole of our British Sheep Breeds yarn range is spun entirely in Yorkshire you will also be supporting the UK yarn spinning industry by buying British.

ecru 220

Rowan Purelife Renew

Following on from the success of Rowan Purelife Revive in Spring 2010, we now see the launch of Rowan's second fully recycled yarn, Renew.

Made from recycled wool, with a fabulous tweedy character and available in 8 rustic shades ranging from a natural stone through to a deep vibrant blue.

The Recycled Wool Process

The origin of the clothes for recycling is varied: unsold goods, used garments, waste of weaving and spinning companies.

- Initial sort of recycled clothes by colour and fibre-quality.
- All linings, buttons, zips, ornaments, seams are removed.
- Further sorting by fibre type and colour and quality. Multicoloured clothes are separately classified as "millefiori". When recycled they create only one colour, a kind of brown with red and white specks, this is then over dyed in black or navy blue.
- The cloth is then sterilised to eliminate any impurities, cut into pieces and introduced into a rag grinder, which reduces them to loose fibres, these fibres are then ready for carding.
- Once carding is finished the fibre then enters the normal spinning process and the yarn is then ready to be knitted again.

tractor 680
trailer 681
digger 682
pick up 683
garage 684
diesel 685
truck 686
lorry 687

acacia
page 26
pattern page 48

amaryllis
page 17
pattern page 49

azara scarf
page 9
pattern page 52

crocus
page 35
pattern page 53

cyclamen
page 28
pattern page 54

daphne
page 38
pattern page 69

erica
page 10
pattern page 56

gorse
page 14
pattern page 57

mahonia
page 4
pattern page 70

periwinkle
page 40
pattern page 59

quince
page 24
pattern page 60

senna
page 30
pattern page 62

snowdrop wrap
page 32
pattern page 66

wild saffron
page 20
pattern page 72

winter aconite
page 6
pattern page 64

winter cherry
page 12
pattern page 67

winter sweet
page 18
pattern page 74

acacia 

main image page 26

SIZE

S	M	L	XL	XXL	
To fit bust					
81-86	91-97	102-107	112-117	122-127	cm
32-34	36-38	40-42	44-46	48-50	in

YARN

Rowan Purelife British Sheep Breeds Boucle

4	5	5	6	7	x100gm

(photographed in Ecru 220)

NEEDLES

1 pair 8mm (no 0) (US 11) needles
8mm (no 0) (US 11) circular needle

EXTRAS – 1 decorative kilt pin ref FG10675 from Bedecked. Please see credits page for contact details.

TENSION

8½ sts and 13 rows to 10 cm measured over rev st st using 8mm (US 11) needles.

BACK

Using 8mm (US 11) needles cast on 40 [44: 48: 54: 60] sts.

Rows 1 and 2: Purl.

Beg with a P row, now work in rev st st until back meas 11 [12: 13: 14: 15] cm, ending with RS facing for next row.

Shape for cap sleeves

Inc 1 st at each end of next and foll 4th row, then on foll alt row, then on foll 2 rows, ending with **WS** facing for next row. 50 [54: 58: 64: 70] sts.

Place markers at both ends of last row to denote base of armhole openings.

Cont straight until armhole meas 20 [21: 22: 23: 24] cm from markers, ending with RS facing for next row.

Shape shoulders and back neck

Cast off 5 [6: 7: 8: 9] sts at beg of next 2 rows. 40 [42: 44: 48: 52] sts.

Next row (RS): Cast off 5 [6: 7: 8: 9] sts, P until there are 9 [9: 9: 10: 11] sts on right needle and turn, leaving rem sts on a holder.

Work each side of neck separately.

Cast off 3 sts at beg of next row.

Cast off rem 6 [6: 6: 7: 8] sts.

With RS facing, rejoin yarn to rem sts, cast off centre 12 sts, P to end.

Complete to match first side, reversing shapings.

LEFT FRONT

Using 8mm (US 11) needles cast on 30 [32: 34: 37: 40] sts.

Rows 1 and 2: Purl.

Beg with a P row, now work in rev st st until left front meas 11 [12: 13: 14: 15] cm, ending with RS facing for next row.

Shape for cap sleeve

Inc 1 st at beg of next and foll 4th row. 32 [34: 36: 39: 42] sts.

Work 1 row, ending with RS facing for next row.

Shape front slope

Dec 1 st at end (front slope edge) of next row and at same edge on foll 2 rows **and at same time** inc 1 st at beg (cap sleeve edge) of next row and at same edge on foll 2 rows, ending with **WS** facing for next row. 32 [34: 36: 39: 42] sts.

Place marker at end of last row to denote base of armhole opening.

Dec 1 st at front slope edge of next 10 [10: 8: 6: 6] rows, then on foll 6 [6: 8: 10: 10] alt rows. 16 [18: 20: 23: 26] sts.

Cont straight until left front matches back to beg of shoulder shaping, ending with RS facing for next row.

Shape shoulder

Cast off 5 [6: 7: 8: 9] sts at beg of next and foll alt row.

Work 1 row.

Cast off rem 6 [6: 6: 7: 8] sts.

RIGHT FRONT

Using 8mm (US 11) needles cast on 30 [32: 34: 37: 40] sts.

Rows 1 and 2: Purl.

Beg with a P row, now work in rev st st until right front meas 11 [12: 13: 14: 15] cm, ending with RS facing for next row.

Shape for cap sleeve

Inc 1 st at end of next and foll 4th row. 32 [34: 36: 39: 42] sts.

Complete to match left front, reversing shapings.

MAKING UP

Press as described on the information page.

Join both shoulder seams using back stitch, or mattress stitch if preferred.

Front band

With RS facing and using 8mm (US 11) circular needle, beg and ending at cast-on edges, pick up and knit 13 [14: 15: 16: 17] sts up right front opening edge to beg of front slope shaping, 26 [26: 28: 30: 30] sts up right front slope, 18 sts from back, 26 [26: 28: 30: 30] sts down left front slope to beg of front slope shaping, then 13 [14: 15: 16: 17] sts down left front opening edge. 96 [98: 104: 110: 112] sts.

Work in g st for 2 rows, ending with **WS** facing for next row.

Cast off knitwise (on **WS**).

Armhole borders (both alike)

With RS facing and using 8mm (US 11) needles, pick up and knit 34 [36: 37: 39: 41] sts evenly along armhole opening edge between markers.

Work in g st for 2 rows, ending with **WS** facing for next row.
Cast off knitwise (on **WS**).
See information page for finishing instructions, fastening fronts with decorative kilt pin as in photograph.

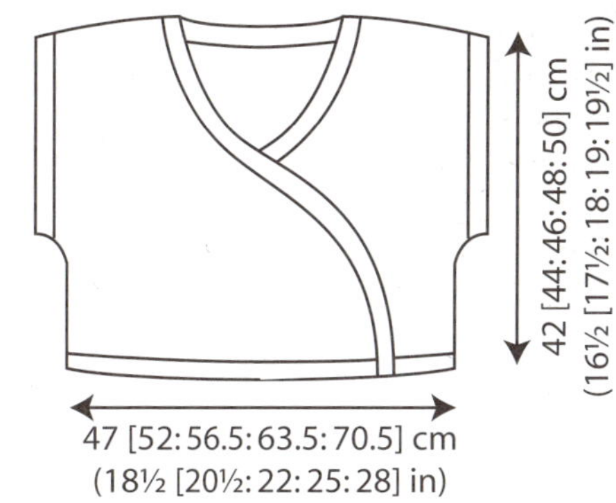

amaryllis

main image page 17

SIZE

S	M	L	XL	XXL	
To fit bust					
81-86	91-97	102-107	112-117	122-127	cm
32-34	36-38	40-42	44-46	48-50	in

YARN

Rowan Purelife British Sheep Breeds Chunky

10	10	11	12	13	x 100gm

(photographed in Shetland Moorit 955)

NEEDLES

1 pair 7mm (no 2) (US 10½) needles
Cable needle

BUTTONS – 5 x FG1067S from Bedecked. Please see credits page for contact details.

TENSION

13 sts and 18 rows to 10 cm measured over st st, 16½ sts and 20 rows to 10 cm measured over cable patt, both using 7mm (US 10½) needles.

SPECIAL ABBREVIATIONS

bind 6 = K2, P2, K2, slip these 6 sts onto cable needle, wrap yarn 4 times anti-clockwise round these 6 sts, then slip these 6 sts back onto right needle; **C4B** = slip next 2 sts onto cable needle and leave at back of work, K2, then K2 from cable needle; **Cr3L** = slip next 2 sts onto cable needle and leave at front of work, P1, then K2 from cable needle; **Cr3R** = slip next st onto cable needle and leave at back of work, K2, then P1 from cable needle.

PEPLUM (worked sideways)

Using 7mm (US 10½) needles cast on 36 [38: 39: 42: 43] sts.

Row 1 (RS): (K1, P1) twice, K to end.
Row 2: P to last 4 sts, (P1, K1) twice.
These 2 rows form peplum patt – lower edge 4 sts in moss st with all other sts in st st.
Cont as set for a further 4 [6: 8: 8: 10] rows, ending with RS facing for next row.

Shape peplum

Row 1 (RS): Patt 30 [31: 32: 35: 35] sts, wrap next st (by slipping next st on left needle onto right needle, taking yarn to opposite side of work between needles and then slipping same st back onto left needle – when working back across wrapped sts, work the wrapped st and the wrapping loop tog as one st) and turn.
Row 2: Patt to end.
Row 3: Patt 24 [24: 25: 28: 28] sts, wrap next st and turn.
Row 4: Patt to end.
Row 5: Patt 18 [18: 18: 21: 21] sts, wrap next st and turn.
Row 6: Patt to end.
Row 7: Patt 12 [12: 12: 14: 14] sts, wrap next st and turn.
Row 8: Patt to end.
Row 9: Patt 6 [6: 6: 7: 7] sts, wrap next st and turn.
Row 10: Patt to end.
These 10 rows complete first set of peplum shaping rows.
Patt 12 [14: 14: 16: 18] rows across all sts.

Next row (RS): *K1, P1, rep from * to last 0 [0: 1: 0: 1] st, K0 [0: 1: 0: 1].
Next row: K0 [0: 1: 0: 1], *P1, K1, rep from * to end.
Last 2 rows form moss st.
Work in moss st for a further 2 rows.
Work in peplum patt for 12 [14: 14: 16: 18] rows.
Work the 10 peplum shaping rows once more.
Work in peplum patt for 6 [7: 8: 9: 10] rows.
Place marker at shorter row-end edge of last row – this denotes base of left side seam.
Work in peplum patt for 4 [5: 8: 9: 10] rows.
Work the 10 peplum shaping rows once more.
Work in peplum patt for 12 [14: 14: 16: 18] rows.
Work in moss st for 4 rows.
Work in peplum patt for 12 [14: 14: 16: 18] rows.
Work the 10 peplum shaping rows once more.
Work in peplum patt for 12 [12: 16: 16: 20] rows.
Work the 10 peplum shaping rows once more.
Work in peplum patt for 12 [14: 14: 16: 18] rows.
Work in moss st for 4 rows.
Work in peplum patt for 12 [14: 14: 16: 18] rows.
Work the 10 peplum shaping rows once more.
Work in peplum patt for 4 [5: 8: 9: 10] rows.
Place marker at shorter row-end edge of last row – this denotes base of right side seam.
Work in peplum patt for 6 [7: 8: 9: 10] rows.
Work the 10 peplum shaping rows once more.
Work in peplum patt for 12 [14: 14: 16: 18] rows.
Work in moss st for 4 rows.
Work in peplum patt for 12 [14: 14: 16: 18] rows.
Work the 10 peplum shaping rows once more.
Work in peplum patt for 6 [8: 10: 10: 12] rows, ending with RS facing for next row.
Cast off.

UPPER BACK

With RS facing and using 7mm (US 10½) needles pick up and knit 70 [78: 88: 98: 110] sts evenly along shorter row-end edge of peplum between markers denoting base of side seams.
Beg and ending rows as indicated, noting that chart row 1 is a **WS** row and repeating the 24 row patt rep throughout, cont in patt from chart for body as folls:
Work 7 rows, ending with RS facing for next row.
Inc 1 st at each end of next and 2 foll 8th rows, taking inc sts into patt. 76 [84: 94: 104: 116] sts.
Cont straight until back meas 46 [47: 48: 49: 50] cm from lower (row-end) edge of peplum, ending with RS facing for next row.

Shape armholes

Keeping patt correct, cast off 3 sts at beg of next 2 rows. 70 [78: 88: 98: 110] sts.
Dec 1 st at each end of next 3 [5: 5: 7: 9] rows, then on foll 2 [3: 5: 6: 7] alt rows. 60 [62: 68: 72: 78] sts.
Cont straight until armhole meas 19 [20: 21: 22: 23] cm, ending with RS facing for next row.

Shape shoulders and back neck

Cast off 5 [5: 6: 7: 7] sts at beg of next 2 rows. 50 [52: 56: 58: 64] sts.
Next row (RS): Cast off 5 [5: 6: 7: 7] sts, patt until there are 8 [9: 9: 9: 11] sts on right needle and turn, leaving rem sts on a holder.
Work each side of neck separately.
Cast off 3 sts at beg of next row.
Cast off rem 5 [6: 6: 6: 8] sts.
With RS facing, rejoin yarn to rem sts, cast off centre 24 [24: 26: 26: 28] sts, patt to end.
Complete to match first side, reversing shapings.

UPPER LEFT FRONT

With RS facing and using 7mm (US 10½) needles pick up and knit 35 [39: 44: 49: 55] sts evenly along shorter row-end edge of peplum from marker denoting base of left side seam to cast-on edge.
Beg and ending rows as indicated, cont in patt from chart for body as folls:
Work 7 rows, ending with RS facing for next row.
Inc 1 st at beg of next and 2 foll 8th rows, taking inc sts into patt. 38 [42: 47: 52: 58] sts.
Cont straight until left front matches back to beg of armhole shaping, ending with RS facing for next row.

Shape armhole

Keeping patt correct, cast off 3 sts at beg of next row. 35 [39: 44: 49: 55] sts.
Work 1 row.
Dec 1 st at armhole edge of next 3 [5: 5: 7: 9] rows, then on foll 2 [2: 2: 1: 0] alt rows. 30 [32: 37: 41: 46] sts.
Work 3 [1: 1: 1: 1] rows, ending with RS facing for next row.

Shape front slope

Keeping patt correct, dec 1 st at end of next row and at same edge on foll 8 [6: 6: 4: 4] rows, then on foll 6 [8: 9: 11: 12] alt rows **and at same time** dec 1 st at armhole edge of
0 [next: next: next: next] and foll 0 [0: 2: 4: 6] alt rows. 15 [16: 18: 20: 22] sts.
Cont straight until left front matches back to beg of shoulder shaping, ending with RS facing for next row.

Shape shoulder

Cast off 5 [5: 6: 7: 7] sts at beg of next and foll alt row.
Work 1 row.
Cast off rem 5 [6: 6: 6: 8] sts.

UPPER RIGHT FRONT

With RS facing and using 7mm (US 10½) needles pick up and knit 35 [39: 44: 49: 55] sts evenly along shorter row-end edge of peplum from cast-on edge to marker denoting base of right side seam.
Beg and ending rows as indicated, cont in patt from chart for body as folls:
Work 7 rows, ending with RS facing for next row.
Inc 1 st at end of next and 2 foll 8th rows, taking inc sts into patt. 38 [42: 47: 52: 58] sts.
Complete to match left front, reversing shapings.

SLEEVES

Using 7mm (UK 10½) needles cast on 37 [39: 41: 41: 43] sts.
Row 1 (RS): K1, *P1, K1, rep from * to end.
Row 2: As row 1.
These 2 rows form moss st.
Work in moss st for a further 3 rows, inc 3 sts evenly across last row and ending with **WS** facing for next row. 40 [42: 44: 44: 46] sts.
Beg and ending rows as indicated, noting that chart row 1 is a **WS** row and repeating the 24 row patt rep throughout, cont in patt from chart for sleeve as folls:
Inc 1 st at each end of 4th and every foll 4th row to 54 [54: 54: 60: 62] sts, then on every foll

6th row until there are 70 [72: 74: 76: 78] sts, taking inc sts into patt.

Cont straight until sleeve meas 46 [47: 48: 48: 48] cm, ending with RS facing for next row.

Shape top

Cast off 3 sts at beg of next 2 rows. 64 [66: 68: 70: 72] sts.

Dec 1 st at each end of next 7 rows, then on every foll alt row until 46 sts rem, then on foll 7 rows, ending with RS facing for next row. 32 sts.

Cast off 4 sts at beg of next 4 rows.

Cast off rem 16 sts.

MAKING UP

Press as described on the information page.

Join both shoulder seams using back stitch, or mattress stitch if preferred.

Left front band and collar

Using 7mm (UK 10½) needles cast on 4 sts.

Row 1 (RS): (K1, P1) twice.

Row 2: (P1, K1) twice.

These 2 rows form moss st.

Cont in moss st until band, when slightly stretched, fits up left front opening edge from lower edge of peplum to a point 8 cm below upper front pick-up row, ending with **WS** facing for next row.

Cast on 4 sts at beg of next row. 8 sts.

Cont in moss st until band, when slightly stretched, fits up left front opening edge to beg of front slope shaping, ending with RS facing for next row.

Shape for collar

Inc 1 st at beg of next and foll 4 alt rows, then on 3 foll 4th rows, taking inc sts into moss st. 16 sts.

Cont straight until collar section, unstretched, fits up left front slope and across to centre back neck, ending with RS facing for next row.

Cast off 6 sts at beg of next and foll alt row.

Work 1 row.

Cast off rem 4 sts.

Slip stitch band and collar in place. Mark positions for 5 buttons on this band – first to come 5 cm below upper front pick-up row,

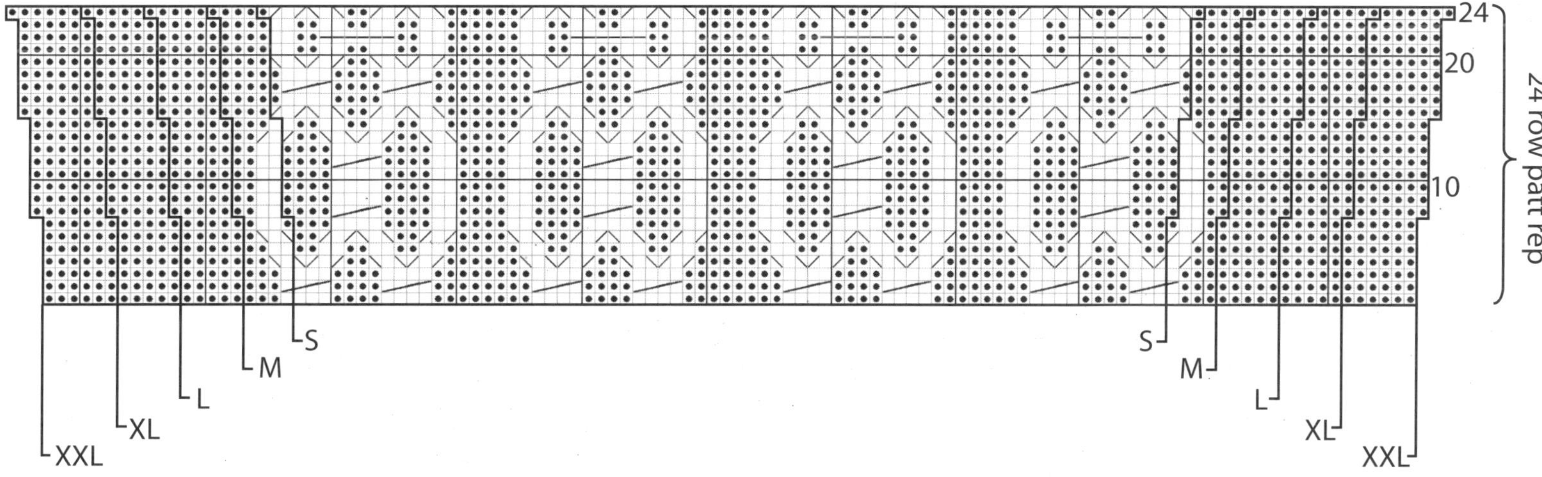

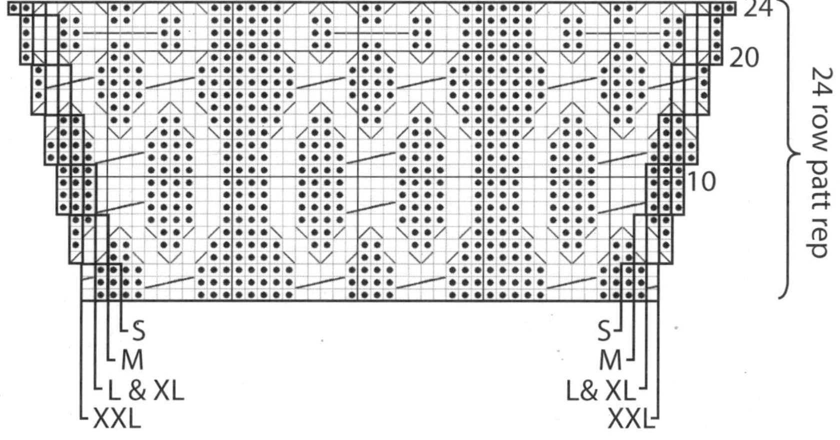

key

(blank square)	K on RS, P on WS
(dot square)	P on RS, K on WS
(symbol)	Cr3R
(symbol)	Cr3L
(symbol)	C4B
(symbol)	bind 6

last to come 1.5 cm below beg of front slope shaping, and rem 3 buttons evenly spaced between.

Right front band and collar

Work as given for left front band and collar, reversing shapings and with the addition of 5 buttonholes worked to correspond with positions marked for buttons as folls:

Buttonhole row (RS): K1, P1, K2tog, yfwd (to make a buttonhole), (K1, P1) twice.

See information page for finishing instructions, setting in sleeves using the set-in method.

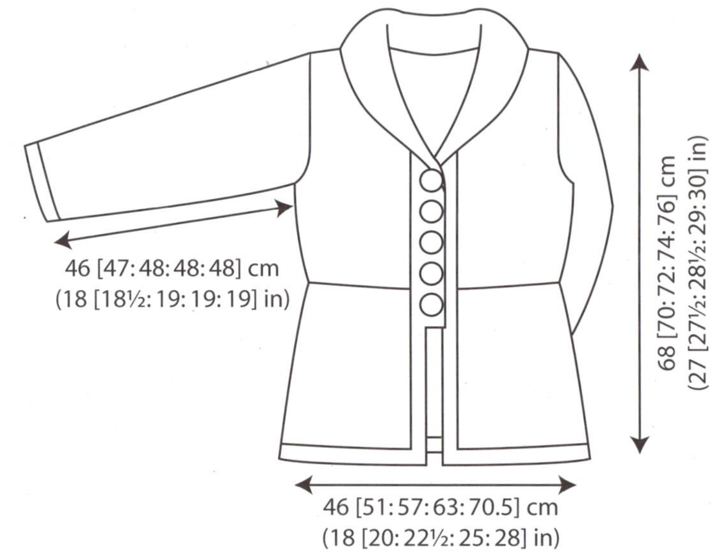

azara scarf

main image page 9

YARN

	short scarf	long scarf	
Rowan Purelife British Sheep Breeds Chunky			
	5	6	x 100gm

(short scarf not photographed, long scarf in Steel Grey Suffolk 954)

NEEDLES

1 pair 8mm (no 0) (US 11) needles

TENSION

9 sts and 18 rows to 10 cm measured over g st using 8mm (US 11) needles.

FINISHED SIZE

Both completed scarves measure 24 cm (9½ ins) wide. Short scarf is 150 cm (59 in) long, and long scarf is 270 cm (106½ in) long.

SCARF

Using 8mm (US 11) needles cast on 22 sts.

Work in g st until scarf meas 150 cm for short scarf, or 270 cm for long scarf, ending with **WS** facing for next row.

Cast off knitwise (on **WS**).

MAKING UP

Do NOT press.

crocus

main image page 35

SIZE

	S	M	L	XL	XXL	
To fit bust						
	81-86	91-97	102-107	112-117	122-127	cm
	32-34	36-38	40-42	44-46	48-50	in

YARN

Rowan Renew

13	13	14	15	16	x 50gm

(photographed in Diesel 685)

NEEDLES

1 pair 6mm (no 4) (US 10) needles
6mm (no 4) (US 10) circular needle

TENSION

18 sts and 22 rows to 10 cm measured over rib using 6mm (US 10) needles.

BODY (worked in one piece, beg at back hem edge)

Using 6mm (US 10) needles cast on 98 [106: 118: 126: 142] sts.

Row 1 (RS): K0 [2: 0: 0: 0], P2, *K2, P2, rep from * to last 0 [2: 0: 0: 0] sts, K0 [2: 0: 0: 0].

Row 2: P0 [2: 0: 0: 0], K2, *P2, K2, rep from * to last 0 [2: 0: 0: 0] sts, P0 [2: 0: 0: 0].

These 2 rows form rib.

Cont in rib for a further 10 rows, ending with RS facing for next row.

Shape sleeves

Changing to 6mm (US 10) circular needle when required and keeping rib correct, cont as folls:

Cast on 7 [8: 7: 6: 6] sts at beg of next 2 [18: 10: 2: 16] rows, then 8 [9: 8: 7: 7] sts at beg of foll 18 [2: 12: 22: 10] rows. 256 [268: 284: 292: 308] sts.

Now working first and last st of every row as a K st and all other sts in rib as set, work 48 [52: 52: 54: 54] rows, placing markers at both ends of 24th [26th: 26th: 27th: 27th] row and ending with RS facing for next row.

Cast off 8 [9: 8: 7: 7] sts at beg of next 18 [2: 12: 22: 10] rows, then 7 [8: 7: 6: 6] sts at beg of foll 2 [18: 10: 2: 16] rows. 98 [106: 118: 126: 142] sts.

Cont in rib for a further 12 rows, ending with RS facing for next row.

Cast off in rib.

COLLAR AND BAND

Using 6mm (US 10) needles cast on 60 sts.

Row 1 (RS): K3, *P2, K2, rep from * to last st, K1.

Row 2: K1, P2, *K2, P2, rep from * to last st, K1.

These 2 rows form rib.

Cont in rib until work meas 109 [118: 131: 140: 158] cm, ending with RS facing for next row.

Cast off in rib.

MAKING UP

Press as described on the information page.

Fold body in half along row with markers at each end and join row-end edges from cast-on and cast-off edges to beg of sleeve shaping (to form side seams) and along shaped sleeve cast-on and cast-off edges (to form sleeve seams) using back stitch, or mattress stitch if preferred. Join cast-on and cast-off edges of collar and band to form one long loop. Matching band seam to centre of body cast-on edge, sew one edge of collar and band loop to cast-on and cast-off edges of body.

See information page for finishing instructions.

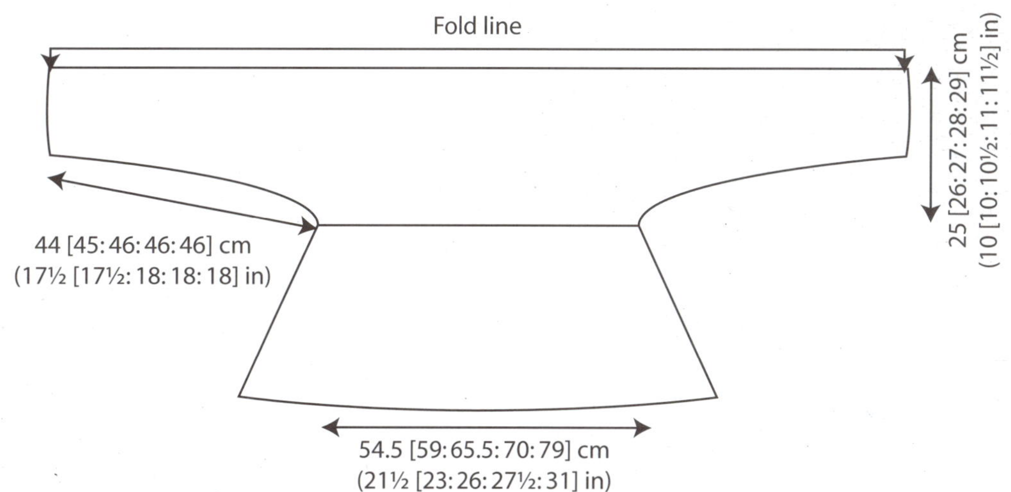

cyclamen

main image page 28

SIZE

S	M	L	XL	XXL	
To fit bust					
81-86	91-97	102-107	112-117	122-127	cm
32-34	36-38	40-42	44-46	48-50	in

YARN

Rowan Renew

9	10	10	11	12	x 50gm

(photographed in Pick Up 683)

NEEDLES

1 pair 6mm (no 4) (US 10) needles

BUTTONS - 2 x RW5030 - 23mm gunmetal, from Bedecked. Please see credits page for contact details.

TENSION

16 sts and 28 rows to 10 cm measured over patt using 6mm (US 10) needles.

SPECIAL ABBREVIATIONS

K1 below = K into st directly below next st on left needle, slipping st above off left needle at same time.

BACK

Using 6mm (US 10) needles cast on 73 [81: 91: 101: 113] sts.

Beg with a RS row, work in g st for 13 rows, ending with **WS** facing for next row.

Now work in patt as folls:

Row 1 (WS): sl 1, *P1, K1 below, rep from * to last 2 sts, P1, K1.

Row 2: sl 1, *K1 below, P1, rep from * to last 2 sts, K1 below, K1.

These 2 rows form patt.

Cont in patt until back meas 20 [21: 22: 23: 24] cm, ending with RS facing for next row.

Shape raglan armholes

Keeping patt correct, cast off 3 sts at beg of next 2 rows. 67 [75: 85: 95: 107] sts.

Dec 1 st at each end of next 1 [1: 1: 3: 9] rows, then on 8 [5: 3: 0: 0] foll 4th rows, then on foll 10 [17: 23: 29: 28] alt rows. 29 [29: 31: 31: 33] sts.

Work 1 row, ending with RS facing for next row.

Cast off.

LEFT FRONT

Using 6mm (US 10) needles cast on 43 [47: 51: 57: 63] sts.

Beg with a RS row, work in g st for 12 rows, ending with RS facing for next row.

Row 13 (RS): K to last 7 sts, M1 and turn, leaving last 7 sts on a holder. 37 [41: 45: 51: 57] sts.

Beg with row 1, work in patt as given for back until left front matches back to beg of raglan armhole shaping, ending with RS facing for next row.

Shape raglan armhole

Keeping patt correct, cast off 3 sts at beg of next row. 34 [38: 42: 48: 54] sts.

Work 1 row.

Dec 1 st at raglan armhole edge of next 1 [1: 1: 3: 9] rows, then on 8 [5: 3: 0: 0] foll 4th rows, then on foll 2 [9: 14: 20: 18] alt rows, ending with **WS** facing for next row. 23 [23: 24: 25: 27] sts.

Shape neck

Keeping patt correct, cast off 11 [11: 10: 11: 11] sts at beg of next row. 12 [12: 14: 14: 16] sts.

Dec 1 st at neck edge of next 5 rows, then on foll 1 [1: 2: 2: 3] alt rows **and at same time** dec 1 st at raglan armhole edge of next and foll 3 [3: 4: 4: 5] alt rows. 2 sts.

Work 1 row, ending with RS facing for next row.

Next row (RS): K2tog and fasten off.

RIGHT FRONT

Using 6mm (US 10) needles cast on 43 [47: 51: 57: 63] sts.

Beg with a RS row, work in g st for 12 rows, ending with RS facing for next row.

Row 13 (RS): K7 and slip these 7 sts onto a holder, M1, K to end. 37 [41: 45: 51: 57] sts.

Beg with row 1, work in patt as given for back and complete to match left front, reversing shapings.

SLEEVES

Using 6mm (US 10) needles cast on 51 [53: 57: 59: 63] sts.

Beg with a RS row, work in g st, shaping sides by inc 1 st at each end of 3rd and 2 foll 4th rows. 57 [59: 63: 65: 69] sts.

Work 2 rows, ending with **WS** facing for next row.

Beg with row 1, cont in patt as given for back as folls:

Work 1 row, ending with RS facing for next row.

Shape raglan

Keeping patt correct, cast off 3 sts at beg of next 2 rows. 51 [53: 57: 59: 63] sts.

Dec 1 st at each end of next and 5 foll 4th rows, then on every foll alt row until 15 sts rem.

Work 1 row, ending with RS facing for next row.

Left sleeve only

Dec 1 st at each end of next row, then cast off 2 sts at beg of foll row. 11 sts.

Dec 1 st at each end of next row, then dec 1 st at beg of foll row. 8 sts.

Right sleeve only

Cast off 2 sts at beg and dec 1 st at end of next row, then dec 1 st at end of foll row. 11 sts.

Dec 1 st at each end of next row, then dec 1 st at end of foll row. 8 sts.

Both sleeves

Rep last 2 rows twice more.

Next row (RS): K2tog and fasten off.

MAKING UP

Press as described on the information page.

Join all raglan seams using back stitch, or mattress stitch if preferred.

Button band

Slip 7 sts on left front holder onto 6mm (US 10) needles and rejoin yarn with RS facing.

Cont in g st until band, when slightly stretched, fits up left front opening edge, ending with **WS** facing for next row.

Cast off knitwise (on **WS**).

Slip stitch band in place. Mark positions for 2 buttons on this band – top button to come 2 cm down from cast-off edge, and other button halfway between this button and cast-on edge.

Buttonhole band

Slip 7 sts on right front holder onto 6mm (US 10) needles and rejoin yarn with **WS** facing.

Cont in g st until band, when slightly stretched, fits up right front opening edge, making 2 buttonholes to correspond with positions marked for buttons as folls:-

Buttonhole row (RS): K2, cast off 2 sts (to make a buttonhole – cast on 2 sts over these cast-off sts on next row), K to end.

When band is complete, ending with **WS** facing for next row, cast off knitwise (on **WS**).

Collar

Using 6mm (US 10) needles cast on 125 [125: 131: 133: 141] sts.

Beg with a RS row, work in g st for 6 rows, ending with RS facing for next row.

Next row (RS): Cast off 12 sts, K to last 12 sts, cast off rem 12 sts.

Break yarn.

With **WS** facing, rejoin yarn to centre 101 [101: 107: 109: 117] sts.

Beg with row 1, cont in patt as given for back until collar meas 6 cm from cast-off edges, ending with RS facing for next row.

Keeping patt correct, cast off 4 sts at beg of next 14 [14: 10: 8: 2] rows, then 5 sts at beg of foll 2 [2: 6: 8: 14] rows.

Cast off rem 35 [35: 37: 37: 39] sts.

Neatly sew cast-off edges of g st sections to row-end edges of patt section. Positioning ends of collar halfway across top of bands, sew shaped cast-off edge of collar to neck edge.

See information page for finishing instructions.

erica

main image page 10

SIZE

S	M	L	XL	XXL	
To fit bust					
81-86	91-97	102-107	112-117	122-127	cm
32-34	36-38	40-42	44-46	48-50	in

YARN

Rowan Purelife British Sheep Breeds Chunky

7	8	9	10	11	x 100gm

(photographed in Steel Grey Suffolk 954)

NEEDLES

1 pair 6mm (no 4) (US 10) needles
1 pair 7mm (no 2) (US 10½) needles
6mm (no 4) (US 10) circular needle
Cable needle

TENSION

16 sts and 18½ rows to 10 cm measured over patt using 7mm (US 10½) needles.

SPECIAL ABBREVIATIONS

C2B = slip next st onto cable needle and leave at back of work, K1, then K1 from cable needle; **C2F** = slip next st onto cable needle and leave at front of work, K1, then K1 from cable needle.

BACK

Using 6mm (US 10) needles cast on 78 [86: 94: 106: 114] sts.
Row 1 (RS): K2, *P2, K2, rep from * to end.
Row 2: P2, *K2, P2, rep from * to end.
These 2 rows form rib.
Work in rib for a further 14 rows, ending with RS facing for next row.
Change to 7mm (US 10 1/2) needles.
Now work in patt as folls:
Row 1 (RS): K1, *C2F, C2B, rep from * to last st, K1.
Row 2: Purl.
Row 3: K1, *C2B, C2F, rep from * to last st, K1.
Row 4: Purl.
These 4 rows form patt.
Cont in patt until back meas 69 [71: 73: 75: 77] cm, ending with RS facing for next row.
Shape shoulders and back neck
Cast off 8 [9: 10: 12: 13] sts at beg of next 2 rows. 62 [68: 74: 82: 88] sts.
Next row (RS): Cast off 8 [9: 10: 12: 13] sts, patt until there are 10 [12: 13: 15: 16] sts on right needle and turn, leaving rem sts on a holder.
Work each side of neck separately.
Cast off 3 sts at beg of next row.
Cast off rem 7 [9: 10: 12: 13] sts.
With RS facing, rejoin yarn to rem sts, cast off centre 26 [26: 28: 28: 30] sts, patt to end.
Complete to match first side, reversing shapings.

FRONT

Work as given for back until front meas 44 [46: 47: 49: 50] cm, ending with RS facing for next row.
Divide for neck
Next row (RS): Patt 39 [43: 47: 53: 57] sts and turn, leaving rem sts on a holder.
Work each side of neck separately.
Keeping patt correct, dec 1 st at neck edge of 2nd and foll 11 [11: 12: 12: 13] alt rows, then on 4 foll 4th rows. 23 [27: 30: 36: 39] sts.
Cont straight until front matches back to beg of shoulder shaping, ending with RS facing for next row.
Shape shoulder
Cast off 8 [9: 10: 12: 13] sts at beg of next and foll alt row.
Work 1 row.
Cast off rem 7 [9: 10: 12: 13] sts.
With RS facing, rejoin yarn to rem sts, patt to end. 39 [43: 47: 53: 57] sts.
Complete to match first side, reversing shapings.

MAKING UP

Press as described on the information page.
Join both shoulder seams using back stitch, or mattress stitch if preferred.
Neckband
With RS facing and using 6mm (US 10) circular needle, beg and ending at base of V neck, pick up and knit 46 [46: 47: 49: 50] sts up right front slope, 32 [32: 34: 34: 36] sts from back, then 46 [46: 47: 49: 50] sts down left front slope. 124 [124: 128: 132: 136] sts.
Row 1 (WS): K1, P2, *K2, P2, rep from * to last st, K1.
Row 2: K3, *P2, K2, rep from * to last st, K1.
These 2 rows form rib.
Work in rib for a further 5 rows, ending with RS facing for next row.
Cast off in rib.
Lay right front end of neckband over left front end as in photograph and neatly sew row-end edges in place.
Mark points along side seam edges 21 [22: 23: 24: 25] cm either side of shoulder seams – these markers denote base of armholes.

Armhole borders (both alike)

With RS facing and using 6mm (US 10) needles, pick up and knit 66 [70: 74: 78: 82] sts evenly along row-end edges between markers.

Beg with row 2, work in rib as given for back for 5 rows, ending with RS facing for next row.

Cast off in rib.

See information page for finishing instructions.

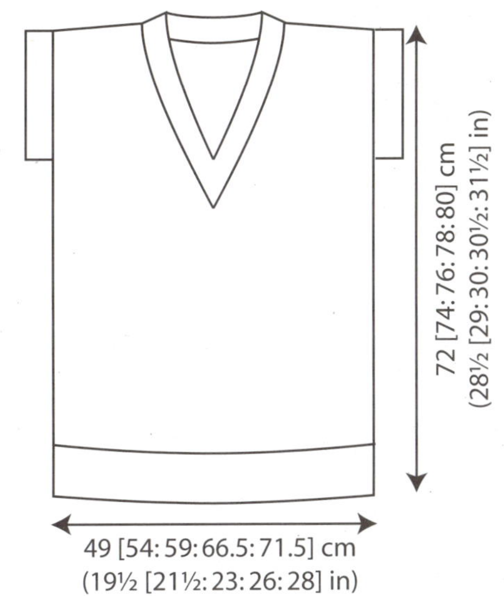

gorse

main image page 14

SIZE

	S	M	L	XL	XXL	
To fit bust						
	81-86	91-97	102-107	112-117	122-127	cm
	32-34	36-38	40-42	44-46	48-50	in

YARN

Rowan Purelife British Sheep Breeds Boucle

11	12	14	15	17	x 100gm

(photographed in Ecru 220)

NEEDLES

1 pair 7mm (no 2) (US 10½) needles

1 pair 8mm (no 0) (US 11) needles

7mm (no 2) (US 10½) circular needle

TENSION

8½ sts and 13 rows to 10 cm measured over rev st st using 8mm (US 11) needles.

BACK

Using 8mm (US 11) needles cast on 45 [49: 55: 59: 65] sts.

Beg with a P row, work in rev st st, shaping side seams by dec 1 st at each end of 21st and foll 20th row. 41 [45: 51: 55: 61] sts.

Cont straight until back meas 50 [51: 52: 53: 54] cm, ending with RS facing for next row.

Shape armholes

Cast off 2 sts at beg of next 2 rows. 37 [41: 47: 51: 57] sts.

Dec 1 st at each end of next 1 [1: 3: 3: 5] rows, then on foll 1 [2: 2: 3: 2] alt rows. 33 [35: 37: 39: 43] sts.

Cont straight until armhole meas 19 [20: 21: 22: 23] cm, ending with RS facing for next row.

Shape back neck and shoulders

Next row (RS): Cast off 3 [4: 4: 5: 5] sts, P until there are 7 [7: 8: 8: 9] sts on right needle and turn, leaving rem sts on a holder.

Work each side of neck separately.

Cast off 3 sts at beg of next row.

Cast off rem 4 [4: 5: 5: 6] sts.

With RS facing, rejoin yarn to rem sts, cast off centre 13 [13: 13: 13: 15] sts, P to end.

Complete to match first side, reversing shapings.

LEFT FRONT

Using 8mm (US 11) needles cast on 23 [25: 28: 30: 33] sts.

Beg with a P row, work in rev st st, shaping side seam by dec 1 st at beg of 21st and foll 20th row. 21 [23: 26: 28: 31] sts.

Cont straight until left front matches back to beg of armhole shaping, ending with RS facing for next row.

Shape armhole

Cast off 2 sts at beg of next row. 19 [21: 24: 26: 29] sts.

Work 1 row.

Dec 1 st at armhole edge of next 1 [1: 2: 2: 2] rows. 18 [20: 22: 24: 27] sts.

Work 1 [1: 0: 0: 0] row, ending with RS facing for next row.

Shape front slope

Dec 1 st at end of next row and at same edge on foll 2 [0: 0: 0: 0] rows, then at end of foll 7 [9: 8: 8: 9] alt rows, then on 0 [0: 1: 1: 1] foll 4th row **and at same time** dec 1 st at armhole edge of next 1 [1: 1: 1: 3] rows, then on foll 0 [1: 2: 3: 2] alt rows. 7 [8: 9: 10: 11] sts.

Cont straight until left front matches back to beg of shoulder shaping, ending with RS facing for next row.

Shape shoulder

Cast off 3 [4: 4: 5: 5] sts at beg of next row.

Work 1 row.

Cast off rem 4 [4: 5: 5: 6] sts.

RIGHT FRONT

Using 8mm (US 11) needles cast on 23 [25: 28: 30: 33] sts.

Beg with a P row, work in rev st st, shaping side seam by dec 1 st at end of 21st and foll 20th row. 21 [23: 26: 28: 31] sts.

Complete to match left front, reversing shapings.

SLEEVES

Using 7mm (US 10½) needles cast on 26 [26: 26: 26: 30] sts.

Row 1 (RS): K2, *P2, K2, rep from * to end.

Row 2: P2, *K2, P2, rep from * to end.

These 2 rows form rib.

Cont in rib, inc 1 st at each end of 5th [5th: 3rd: 3rd: 3rd] and 1 [1: 1: 2: 2] foll 8th [8th: 8th: 6th: 6th] rows, taking inc sts into rib. 30 [30: 30: 32: 36] sts.

Work a further 3 [3: 5: 1: 1] rows, dec 3 [1: 1: 1: 3] sts evenly across last row and ending with RS facing for next row. 27 [29: 29: 31: 33] sts.

Change to 8mm (US 11) needles.

Beg with a P row, now work in rev st st, shaping sides by inc 1 st at each end of 5th [5th: 3rd: 5th: 5th] and every foll 8th [8th: 8th: 6th: 6th] row to 33 [33: 39: 35: 37] sts, then on every foll 10th [10th: -: 8th: 8th] row until there are 35 [37: -: 41: 43] sts.

Cont straight until sleeve meas 44 [45: 46: 46: 46] cm, ending with RS facing for next row.

Shape top

Cast off 2 sts at beg of next 2 rows. 31 [33: 35: 37: 39] sts.

Dec 1 st at each end of next 3 rows, then on every foll alt row until there are 21 sts, then on foll 5 rows, ending with RS facing for next row.

Cast off rem 11 sts.

MAKING UP

Press as described on the information page.

Join both shoulder seams using back stitch, or mattress stitch if preferred.

Front band

With RS facing and using 7mm (US 10½) circular needle, beg and ending at cast-on edges, pick up and knit 45 [46: 47: 48: 49] sts up right front opening edge to beg of front slope shaping, 20 [22: 23: 24: 26] sts up right front slope, 18 [20: 20: 20: 22] sts from back, 20 [22: 23: 24: 26] sts down left front slope to beg of front slope shaping, then 45 [46: 47: 48: 49] sts down left front opening edge. 148 [156: 160: 164: 172] sts.

Row 1 (WS): K1, P2, *K2, P2, rep from * to last st, K1.

Row 2: K3, *P2, K2, rep from * to last st, K1.

These 2 rows form rib.

Work in rib until front band meas 12 cm, ending with RS facing for next row.

Cast off in rib.

See information page for finishing instructions, setting in sleeves using the set-in method.

Belt

Using 7mm (US 10½) needles cast on 6 sts.

Row 1 (RS): K2, P2, K2.

Row 2: P2, K2, P2.

These 2 rows form rib.

Cont in rib until belt meas 150 [160: 170: 180: 190] cm, ending with RS facing for next row.

Cast off in rib.

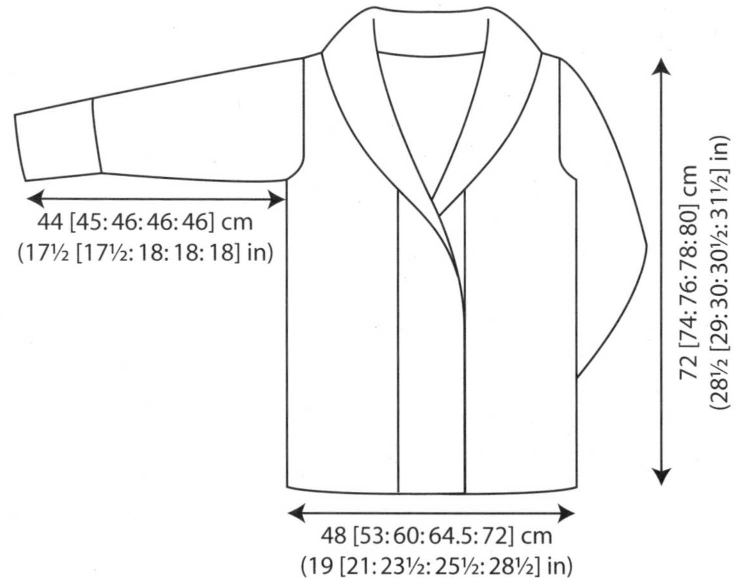

periwinkle

main image page 40

YARN

	S-M	L-XL	XXL	
To fit bust				
	81-97	102-117	122-127	cm
	32-38	40-46	48-50	in

YARN

Rowan Renew

9	10	10	x 50gm

(photographed in Lorry 687)

NEEDLES

1 pair 6mm (no 4) (US 10) needles

TENSION

15 sts and 21 rows to 10 cm measured over patt using 6mm (US 10) needles.

SPECIAL ABBREVIATIONS

K1 below = K into st directly below next st on left needle, slipping st above off left needle at same time.

BLOCKS (make 8)

Using 6mm (US 10) needles cast on 45 [53: 59] sts.

Row 1 (WS): K6 [8: 8], (P7 [7: 9], K6 [8: 8]) 3 times.

Now work in patt as folls:

Row 1 (RS): P6 [8: 8], *(K1 below, P1) 3 [3: 4] times, K1 below, P6 [8: 8], rep from * twice more.

Row 2: K6 [8: 8], *(P1, K1 below) 3 [3: 4] times, P1, K6 [8: 8], rep from * twice more.

These 2 rows form patt.

Cont in patt until block meas 29 [35: 39] cm, ending with RS facing for next row. (Block should be a square.)

Cast off in patt.

MAKING UP

Press as described on the information page.

Following diagram, join 4 blocks together to form a square using back stitch, or mattress stitch if preferred, leaving 19 [20: 21] cm opening at top of centre seam – this forms front. Leaving centre seam open, join rem 4 blocks in same way for back. Mark points along centre back seam 5 cm down from upper edges. Join both shoulder seams.

Neck trim

With RS facing and using 6mm (US 10) needles, beg and ending at marked points on back, pick up and knit 34 [35: 36] sts down left side of neck slit to top of centre front seam, then 34 [35: 36] sts up right side of neck slit. 68 [70: 72] sts.

Cast off knitwise (on **WS**).

Join centre back and neck trim seam.

Armhole borders (both alike)

Mark points along side seam edges 24 [26: 27] cm either side of shoulder seams.

With RS facing and using 6mm (US 10) needles, pick up and knit 67 [73: 75] sts evenly along armhole edge between marked points.

Cast off knitwise (on **WS**).

Hem trim (both alike)

With RS facing and using 6mm (US 10) needles, pick up and knit 81 [98: 109] sts evenly along lower edge of front.

Cast off knitwise (on **WS**).

Work hem trim across lower edge of back in same way.

See information page for finishing instructions.

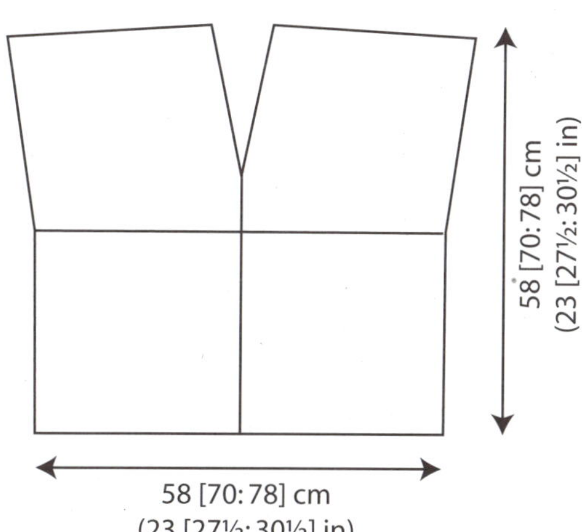

quince

main image page 24

SIZE

S	M	L	XL	XXL	
To fit bust					
81-86	91-97	102-107	112-117	122-127	cm
32-34	36-38	40-42	44-46	48-50	in

YARN

Rowan Purelife British Sheep Breeds Boucle

8	9	9	10	11	x 100gm

(photographed in Ecru 220)

NEEDLES

1 pair 7mm (no 2) (US 10½) needles
1 pair 8mm (no 0) (US 11) needles
7mm (no 2) (US 10½) circular needle
Cable needle

TENSION

8½ sts and 13 rows to 10 cm measured over rev st st using 8mm (US 11) needles.

SPECIAL ABBREVIATIONS

C4B = slip next 2 sts onto cable needle and leave at back of work, K2, then K2 from cable needle; **C4F** = slip next 2 sts onto cable needle and leave at front of work, K2, then K2 from cable needle; **Cr3L** = slip next 2 sts onto cable needle and leave at front of work, P1, then K2 from cable needle; **Cr3R** = slip next st onto cable needle and leave at back of work, K2, then P1 from cable needle.

BACK

Using 7mm (US 10½) needles cast on 49 [53: 57: 63: 69] sts.

Row 1 (RS): K2 [0: 0: 0: 0], P3 [1: 3: 0: 3], *K3, P3, rep from * to last 2 [4: 0: 3: 0] sts, K2 [3: 0: 3: 0], P0 [1: 0: 0: 0].

Row 2: P2 [0: 0: 0: 0], K3 [1: 3: 0: 3], *P3, K3, rep from * to last 2 [4: 0: 3: 0] sts, P2 [3: 0: 3: 0], K0 [1: 0: 0: 0].

These 2 rows form rib.

Cont in rib for a further 10 rows, dec 1 st at each end of 7th row and ending with RS facing for next row. 47 [51: 55: 61: 67] sts.

Row 13 (RS): Rib 22 [24: 26: 29: 32], M1, rib 3, M1, rib 22 [24: 26: 29: 32]. 49 [53: 57: 63: 69] sts.

Change to 8mm (US 11) needles.

Now work in patt as folls:

Row 1 (WS): K21 [23: 25: 28: 31], P4, K2, P2, K to end.

Row 2: P2tog, P18 [20: 22: 25: 28], Cr3L, Cr3R, Cr3L, P to last 2 sts, P2tog. 47 [51: 55: 61: 67] sts.

Row 3: K19 [21: 23: 26: 29], P2, K2, P4, K to end.

Row 4: P20 [22: 24: 27: 30], C4B, P2, K2, P to end.

Row 5: As row 3.

Row 6: P19 [21: 23: 26: 29], Cr3R, Cr3L, Cr3R, P to end.

Row 7: K20 [22: 24: 27: 30], P4, K2, P2, K to end.

Row 8: P2tog, P17 [19: 21: 24: 27], K2, P2, C4F, P to last 2 sts, P2tog. 45 [49: 53: 59: 65] sts.

These 8 rows form patt and cont side seam shaping.

Cont in patt, dec 1 st at each end of 6th row. 43 [47: 51: 57: 63] sts.

Cont straight until back meas 27 [27: 27: 29: 30] cm, ending with RS facing for next row.

Shape raglan armholes

Keeping patt correct, cast off 2 sts at beg of next 2 rows. 39 [43: 47: 53: 59] sts.

Dec 1 st at each end of next 1 [1: 1: 7: 11] rows, then on 1 [0: 0: 0: 0] foll 4th row, then on foll 7 [10: 11: 8: 7] alt rows. 21 [21: 23: 23: 23] sts.

Work 1 row, ending with RS facing for next row.

Cast off.

FRONT

Work as given for back until 23 [23: 25: 25: 25] sts rem in raglan armhole shaping.

Work 1 row, ending with RS facing for next row.

Cast off.

SLEEVES

Using 7mm (US 10½) needles cast on 29 [29: 31: 31: 31] sts.

Row 1 (RS): P1 [1: 2: 2: 2], *K3, P3, rep from * to last 4 [4: 5: 5: 5] sts, K3, P1 [1: 2: 2: 2].

Row 2: K1 [1: 2: 2: 2], *P3, K3, rep from * to last 4 [4: 5: 5: 5] sts, P3, K1 [1: 2: 2: 2].

These 2 rows form rib.

Cont in rib for a further 10 rows, inc 0 [1: 1: 1: 1] st at each end of 0 [9th: 9th: 9th: 7th] row and ending with RS facing for next row. 29 [31: 33: 33: 33] sts.

Row 13 (RS): Rib 13 [14: 15: 15: 15], M1, rib 3, M1, rib 13 [14: 15: 15: 15]. 31 [33: 35: 35: 35] sts.

Change to 8mm (US 11) needles.

Now work in patt as folls:

Row 1 (WS): K12 [13: 14: 14: 14], P4, K2, P2, K to

end.

Row 2: (Inc in first st) 1 [0: 0: 0: 0] times, P10 [12: 13: 13: 13], Cr3L, Cr3R, Cr3L, P to last 1 [0: 0: 0: 0] st, (inc in last st) 1 [0: 0: 0: 0] times. 33 [33: 35: 35: 35] sts.

Row 3: K12 [12: 13: 13: 13], P2, K2, P4, K to end.

Row 4: P13 [13: 14: 14: 14], C4B, P2, K2, P to end.

Row 5: As row 3.

Row 6: (Inc in first st) 0 [0: 0: 0: 1] times, P12 [12: 13: 13: 12], Cr3R, Cr3L, Cr3R, P to last 0 [0: 0: 0: 1] st, (inc in last st) 0 [0: 0: 0: 1] times. 33 [33: 35: 35: 37] sts.

Row 7: K13 [13: 14: 14: 15], P4, K2, P2, K to end.

Row 8: P12 [12: 13: 13: 14], K2, P2, C4F, P to end.

These 8 rows form patt and cont sleeve shaping.

Cont in patt, shaping sides by inc 1 st at each end of 10th [2nd: 4th: 4th: 8th] and every foll 18th [14th: 14th: 14th: 12th] row until there are 37 [39: 41: 41: 43] sts, taking inc sts into rev st st.

Cont straight until sleeve meas 44 [45: 46: 46: 46] cm, ending with RS facing for next row.

Shape raglan

Keeping patt correct, cast off 2 sts at beg of next 2 rows. 33 [35: 37: 37: 39] sts.

Dec 1 st at each end of next 3 rows, then on every foll alt row until 13 sts rem.

Work 1 row, ending with RS facing for next row.

Left sleeve only

Dec 1 st at each end of next row, then cast off 5 sts at beg of foll row.

Right sleeve only

Cast off 6 sts at beg and dec 1 st at end of next row.

Work 1 row.

Both sleeves

Cast off rem 6 sts.

MAKING UP

Press as described on the information page.

Join all raglan seams using back stitch, or mattress stitch if preferred.

Collar

With RS facing and using 7mm (US 10½) circular needle, pick up and knit 11 sts from top of left sleeve, 20 [20: 23: 23: 23] sts from front, 11 sts from top of right sleeve, then 18 [18: 21: 21: 21] sts from back. 60 [60: 66: 66: 66] sts.

Round 1 (RS): *K3, P3, rep from * to end.

Rep last round until collar meas 6 cm.

Cast off in rib.

See information page for finishing instructions.

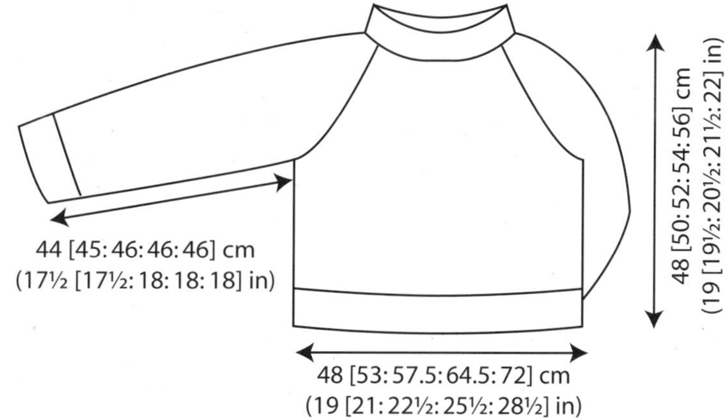

senna

main image page 30

SIZE

S	M	L	XL	XXL	
To fit bust					
81-86	91-97	102-107	112-117	122-127	cm
32-34	36-38	40-42	44-46	48-50	in

YARN

Rowan Renew

12	14	16	17	20	x 50gm

(photographed in Trailer 681)

NEEDLES

1 pair 6mm (no 4) (US 10) needles
2 double-pointed 6mm (no 4) (US 10) needles

TENSION

14 sts and 20 rows to 10 cm measured over st st using 6mm (US 10) needles.

BACK

Using 6mm (US 10) needles cast on 75 [83: 91: 99: 109] sts.

Beg with a RS row, work in g st, dec 1 st at each end of 25th and 2 foll 14th rows. 69 [77: 85: 93: 103] sts.

Work 11 rows, ending with RS facing for next row.

Next row (RS): K1, (P2, K2) 3 times, P2, K to last 15 sts, P2, (K2, P2) 3 times, K1.

Next row: P1, (K2, P2) 3 times, K2, P to last 15 sts, K2, (P2, K2) 3 times, P1.

These 2 rows set the sts – side seam sts in rib with centre sts in st st.

Keeping sts correct as set, dec 1 st at each end of next and 4 foll 8th rows, then on 2 foll 6th row. 55 [63: 71: 79: 89] sts.

Work 13 rows, ending with RS facing for next row.

Inc 1 st at each end of next and 2 foll 10th rows, taking inc sts into rib. 61 [69: 77: 85: 95] sts.

Cont straight until back meas 69 [70: 71: 72: 73] cm, ending with RS facing for next row.

Shape raglan armholes

Keeping sts correct, cast off 3 sts at beg of next 2 rows. 55 [63: 71: 79: 89] sts.

Dec 1 st at each end of next 1 [1: 5: 11: 17] rows, then on 3 [0: 0: 0: 0] foll 4th rows, then on foll 11 [18: 17: 15: 13] alt rows.

25 [25: 27: 27: 29] sts.

Work 1 row, ending with RS facing for next row.

Cast off.

LEFT FRONT

Using 6mm (US 10) needles cast on 39 [43: 47: 51: 56] sts.

Beg with a RS row, work in g st, dec 1 st at beg of 25th and 2 foll 14th rows.

36 [40: 44: 48: 53] sts.

Work 10 rows, ending with **WS** facing for next row.

Next row (WS): K2, M1, K to end.

37 [41: 45: 49: 54] sts.

Next row: K1, (P2, K2) 3 times, P2, K to last 3 sts, P1, K2.

Next row: K1, P1, K1, P to last 15 sts, K2, (P2, K2) 3 times, P1.

Last 2 rows set the sts.

Keeping sts correct as set, dec 1 st at beg of next and 4 foll 8th rows, then on 2 foll 6th row. 30 [34: 38: 42: 47] sts.

Work 7 rows, ending with RS facing for next row.

Next row (RS): Patt to last 9 sts, (P1, K1) 4 times, K1.

Next row: K1, (P1, K1) 4 times, patt to end.

These 2 rows set the sts for rest of left front.

Keeping sts correct as now set, work 4 rows, ending with RS facing for next row.

Inc 1 st at beg of next and 2 foll 10th rows, taking inc sts into rib. 33 [37: 41: 45: 50] sts.

Cont straight until left front matches back to beg of raglan armhole shaping, ending with RS facing for next row.

Shape raglan armhole

Keeping sts correct, cast off 3 sts at beg of next row. 30 [34: 38: 42: 47] sts.

Work 1 row.

Dec 1 st at raglan armhole edge of next 1 [1: 4: 4: 4] rows, then on foll 0 [1: 0: 0: 0] alt row. 29 [32: 34: 38: 43] sts.

Work 3 [1: 0: 0: 0] rows, ending with RS facing for next row.

Shape front slope

Keeping sts correct, dec 1 st at end of next row and at same edge of foll 10 [8: 8: 6: 6] rows, then on foll 6 [8: 9: 11: 12] alt rows **and at same time** dec 1 st at raglan armhole edge of next 1 [1: 1: 7: 13] rows, then on 2 [0: 0: 0: 0] foll 4th rows, then on foll 7 [12: 13: 11: 9] alt rows. 2 sts.

Work 1 row, ending with RS facing for next row.

Next row (RS): K2tog and fasten off.

RIGHT FRONT

Using 6mm (US 10) needles cast on 39 [43: 47: 51: 56] sts.

Beg with a RS row, work in g st, dec 1 st at end of 25th and 2 foll 14th rows. 36 [40: 44: 48: 53] sts.

Work 10 rows, ending with **WS** facing for next row.

Next row (WS): K to last 2 sts, M1, K2. 37 [41: 45: 49: 54] sts.

Next row: K2, P1, K to last 15 sts, P2, (K2, P2) 3

times, K1.

Next row: P1, (K2, P2) 3 times, K2, P to last 3 sts, K1, P1, K1.

Last 2 rows set the sts.

Keeping sts correct as set, dec 1 st at end of next and 4 foll 8th rows, then on 2 foll 6th row. 30 [34: 38: 42: 47] sts.

Work 7 rows, ending with RS facing for next row.

Next row (RS): K1, (K1, P1) 4 times, patt to end.

Next row: Patt to last 9 sts, (K1, P1) 4 times, K1.

These 2 rows set the sts for rest of right front.

Complete to match left front, reversing shapings.

SLEEVES

Using 6mm (US 10) needles cast on 45 [47: 49: 51: 53] sts.

Beg with a RS row, work in g st, inc 1 st at each end of 3rd and foll 2 alt rows. 51 [53: 55: 57: 59] sts.

Work 1 row, ending with RS facing for next row.

Shape raglan

Beg with a K row, cont in st st as folls:

Cast off 3 sts at beg of next 2 rows. 45 [47: 49: 51: 53] sts.

Dec 1 st at each end of next 3 rows, then on every foll alt row until 15 sts rem.

Work 1 row, ending with RS facing for next row.

Left sleeve only

Dec 1 st at each end of next row, then cast off 2 sts at beg of foll row. 11 sts.

Dec 1 st at each end of next row, then dec 1 st at beg of foll row. 8 sts.

Right sleeve only

Cast off 2 sts at beg and dec 1 st at end of next row, then dec 1 st at end of foll row. 11 sts.

Dec 1 st at each end of next row, then dec 1 st at end of foll row. 8 sts.

Both sleeves

Rep last 2 rows twice more. 2 sts.

Next row (RS): K2tog and fasten off.

MAKING UP

Press as described on the information page.

Join all raglan seams using back stitch, or mattress stitch if preferred.

Collar

With RS facing and using 6mm (US 10) needles, beg and ending at beg of front slope shaping, pick up and knit 24 [26: 28: 30: 32] sts up right front slope, 9 sts from top of right sleeve, 24 [26: 28: 27: 29] sts from back, 9 sts from top of left sleeve, then 24 [26: 28: 30: 32] sts down left front slope.

90 [96: 102: 105: 111] sts.

Row 1 (RS of collar, WS of body): K2, P1, inc knitwise in next st, *K1, P1, inc knitwise in next st, rep from * to last 2 sts, K2. 119 [127: 135: 139: 147] sts.

Row 2: K1, *P1, K1, rep from * to end.

Row 3: K2, *P1, K1, rep from * to last st, K1.

Rep last 2 rows until collar meas 5 cm, ending with RS of collar facing for next row.

Next row (RS of collar): Knit.

Next row: K1, P to last st, K1.

Rep last 2 rows once more.

Cast off knitwise.

Pockets (make 2)

Using 6mm (US 10) needles cast on 21 [21: 23: 23: 24] sts.

Row 1 (RS): Knit.

Row 2: K1, P to last st, K1.

Rep last 2 rows until pocket meas 13 [13: 14: 14: 15] cm, ending with RS facing for next row.

Work in g st for 5 rows, ending with **WS** facing for next row.

Cast off knitwise (on **WS**).

Using photograph as a guide, sew pockets onto fronts.

See information page for finishing instructions.

Belt

Using double-pointed 6mm (US 10) needles cast on 4 sts.

Row 1 (RS): K4, *without turning slip these 4 sts to opposite end of needle and bring yarn to opposite end of work pulling it quite tightly across **WS** of work, K these 4 sts again, rep from * until belt meas 150 [160: 170: 180: 190] cm.

Cast off.

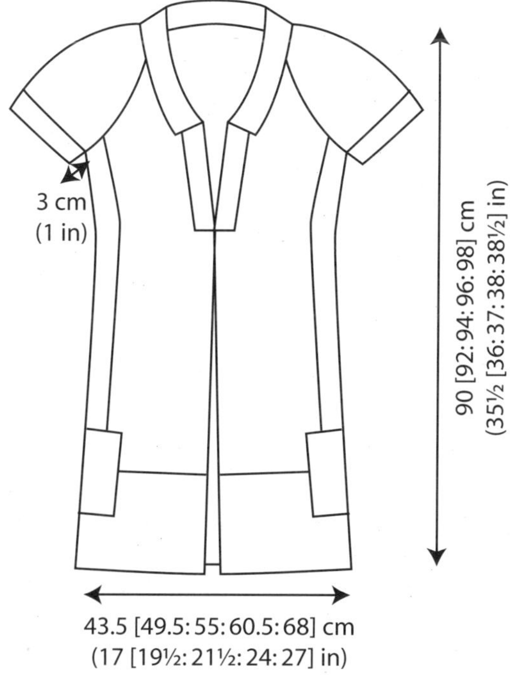

winter aconite 

main image page 6

YARN

	S	M	L	XL	XXL	
To fit bust						
	81-86	91-97	102-107	112-117	122-127	cm
	32-34	36-38	40-42	44-46	48-50	in

YARN

Rowan Renew

18	19	20	22	23	x 50gm

(photographed in Tractor 680)

NEEDLES

1 pair 6mm (no 4) (US 10) needles

Cable needle

BUTTONS – 4 x RW5030 - 23mm gunmetal, from Bedecked. Please see credits page for contact details.

TENSION

16 sts and 24 rows to 10 cm measured over moss st using 6mm (US 10) needles.

Yoke cable panel (32 sts) measures 16 cm.

SPECIAL ABBREVIATIONS

C4B = slip next 2 sts onto cable needle and leave at back of work, K2, then K2 from cable needle; **C4F** = slip next 2 sts onto cable needle and leave at front of work, K2, then K2 from cable needle; **Cr3L** = slip next 2 sts onto cable needle and leave at front of work, P1, then K2 from cable needle; **Cr3R** = slip next st onto cable needle and leave at back of work, K2, then P1 from cable needle; **Cr4L** = slip next 2 sts onto cable needle and leave at front of work, P2, then K2 from cable needle; **Cr4R** = slip next 2 sts onto cable needle and leave at back of work, K2, then P2 from cable needle.

YOKE

Using 6mm (US 10) needles cast on 32 sts.

Sizes M and XL only

Work rows 27 to 32 of chart for yoke, ending with RS facing for next row.

All sizes

Work all 32 rows of chart for yoke 9 [9: 10: 10: 11] times, ending with RS facing for next row.

Now work rows 1 to 2 [8: 2: 8: 2] of chart for yoke once more, ending with RS facing for next row.

Cast off.

Place markers along one edge of yoke strip as folls: place blue markers 18 [19: 20.5: 22: 24] cm in from each end – edge between blue marker and end of strip is upper edge of each front. Mark centre point of strip, then place red markers 18 [19: 20.5: 22: 24] cm either side of centre point – edge between red markers is upper edge of back. Edges between red and blue marker is upper edge of sleeve.

BACK (worked downwards)

With RS facing and using 6mm (US 10) needles pick up and knit 57 [61: 65: 71: 77] sts evenly along row-end edge of yoke between red markers.

Row 1 (WS): K1, *P1, K1, rep from * to end.

This row forms moss st.

Row 2: Inc in first st, moss st 13 [15: 15: 17: 19] sts, place marker on needle, (K1, P1, K1) all into next st, place marker on needle, moss st 27 [27: 31: 33: 35] sts, place marker on needle, (K1, P1, K1) all into next st, place marker on needle, moss st 13 [15: 15: 17: 19] sts, inc in last st. 63 [67: 71: 77: 83] sts, 4 markers in total with 3 sts between each pair of markers.

Work 1 row.

Row 4: Inc in first st, *moss st to marker, slip marker onto right needle, (K1, P1, K1) all into next st, P1, (K1, P1, K1) all into next st, slip marker onto right needle, rep from * once more, moss st to last st, inc in last st. 73 [77: 81: 87: 93] sts, 7 sts between each pair of markers.

Work 1 row.

Row 6: Inc in first st, *moss st to marker, slip marker onto right needle, **(K1, P1, K1) all into next st, P1, rep from ** twice more, (K1, P1, K1) all into next st, slip marker onto right needle, rep from * once more, moss st to last st, inc in last st. 91 [95: 99: 105: 111] sts, 15 sts between each pair of markers.

Remove all 4 markers and cont in moss st as folls:

Inc 1 st at each end of 2nd and foll 0 [3: 4: 4: 3] alt rows, then on 1 [0: 0: 0: 0] foll 4th row, then on foll 0 [0: 2: 4: 8] rows. 95 [103: 113: 123: 135] sts.

Cast on 3 sts at beg of next 2 rows. 101 [109: 119: 129: 141] sts.

Cont straight until back meas 38 [39: 40: 41: 42] cm from last set of cast-on sts, ending with RS facing for next row.

Cast off in moss st.

LEFT FRONT (worked downwards)

With RS facing and using 6mm (US 10) needles pick up and knit 29 [31: 33: 35: 39] sts evenly along row-end edge of yoke between one end of strip and blue marker before back section.

Work in moss st as given for back for 1 row.

Row 2 (RS): Moss st 14 [14: 16: 16: 18] sts, place marker on needle, (K1, P1, K1) all into next st, place marker on needle, moss st 13 [15: 15: 17: 19] sts, inc in last st. 32 [34: 36: 38: 42] sts, 2 markers in total with 3 sts between markers.

Work 1 row.

Row 4: Moss st to marker, slip marker onto right needle, (K1, P1, K1) all into next st, P1, (K1, P1, K1) all into next st, slip marker onto right needle, moss st to last st, inc in last st. 37 [39: 41: 43: 47] sts, 7 sts between markers.

Work 1 row.

Row 6: Moss st to marker, slip marker onto right needle, **(K1, P1, K1) all into next st, P1, rep from ** twice more, (K1, P1, K1) all into next st, slip marker onto right needle, moss st to last st, inc in last st. 46 [48: 50: 52: 56] sts, 15 sts between markers.

Remove both markers and cont in moss st as folls:

Inc 1 st at end of 2nd and foll 0 [3: 4: 4: 3] alt rows, then on 1 [0: 0: 0: 0] foll 4th row, then at same edge on foll 0 [0: 2: 4: 8] rows. 48 [52: 57: 61: 68] sts.

Work 1 row, ending with **WS** facing for next row.

Cast on 3 sts at beg of next row.

51 [55: 60: 64: 71] sts.

Cont straight until left front meas 38 [39: 40: 41: 42] cm from cast-on sts, ending with RS facing for next row.

Cast off in moss st.

RIGHT FRONT (worked downwards)

With RS facing and using 6mm (US 10) needles pick up and knit 29 [31: 33: 35: 39] sts evenly along rem row-end edge of yoke between blue marker after back section and other end of strip.

Work in moss st as given for back for 1 row.

Row 2 (RS): Inc in first st, moss st 13 [15: 15: 17: 19] sts, place marker on needle, (K1, P1, K1) all into next st, place marker on needle, moss st 14 [14: 16: 16: 18] sts. 32 [34: 36: 38: 42] sts, 2 markers in total with 3 sts between markers.

Complete to match left front, reversing shapings.

SLEEVES (worked downwards)

With RS facing and using 6mm (US 10) needles pick up and knit 53 [55: 57: 57: 59] sts evenly along row-end edge of yoke between back and one front.

Work in moss st as given for back for 1 row.

Cont in moss st, inc 1 st at each end of next and foll 5 [4: 2: 3: 2] alt rows, then on 0 [1: 3: 3: 4] foll 4th rows. 65 [67: 69: 71: 73] sts.

Work 1 row, ending with RS facing for next row.

Cast on 3 sts at beg of next 2 rows. 71 [73: 75: 77: 79] sts.

Work 8 [8: 8: 6: 6] rows, ending with RS facing for next row.

Dec 1 st at each end of next and 3 [2: 6: 1: 1] foll 8th [8th: 8th: 6th: 6th] rows, then on 3 [4: 1: 7: 7] foll 10th [10th: 10th: 8th: 8th] rows. 57 [59: 59: 59: 61] sts.

Cont straight until sleeve meas 30 [31: 32: 32: 32] cm from last set of cast-on sts, ending with RS facing for next row.

Cast off in moss st.

MAKING UP

Press as described on the information page.

Join all raglan seams using back stitch, or mattress stitch if preferred.

Collar

With RS facing and using 6mm (US 10) needles, pick up and knit 144 [150: 162: 168: 174] sts evenly along entire free row-end edge of yoke (this is approx 1 st for every 2 rows).

Row 1 (WS): *P2tog, P1, rep from * to end. 96 [100: 108: 112: 116] sts.

Row 2: K1, *P2, K2, rep from * to last 3 sts, P2, K1.

Row 3: K3, *P2, K2, rep from * to last st, K1.

Last 2 rows form rib.

Cont in rib until collar meas 28 cm, ending with RS of collar (**WS** of body) facing for next row.

Cast off loosely in rib.

Button band

Using 6mm (US 10) needles cast on 54 sts, then using same needle and with RS facing pick up and knit 114 [118: 122: 126: 130] sts evenly down left front opening edge from collar pick-up row to cast-off edge of left front. 168 [172: 176: 180: 184] sts.

Beg with row 2, work in rib as given for collar for 1 row, ending with RS facing for next row.

Row 2 (RS of body): Rib 3, yrn, work 2 tog (to make first collar buttonhole), rib 24, yrn, work 2 tog (to make 2nd collar buttonhole), rib to end.

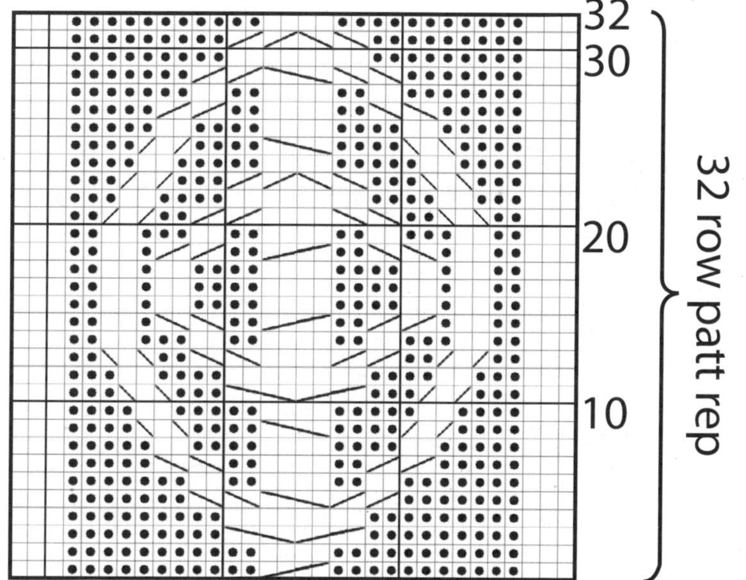

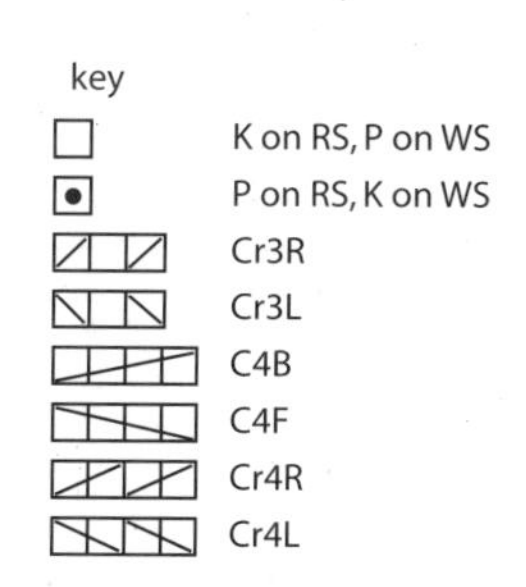

Work in rib for a further 3 rows, ending with RS facing for next row.
Cast off in rib.

Buttonhole band

Using 6mm (US 10) needles and with RS facing pick up and knit 114 [118: 122: 126: 130] sts evenly up right front opening edge from cast-off edge of right front to collar pick-up row, turn and cast on 54 sts. 168 [172: 176: 180: 184] sts.

Beg with row 2, work in rib as given for collar for 1 row, ending with RS facing for next row.

Row 2 (RS of body): Rib 84 [88: 92: 96: 100], yrn, work 2 tog (to make lowest buttonhole), rib 24, yrn, work 2 tog (to make last buttonhole), rib to end.

Work in rib for a further 3 rows, ending with RS facing for next row.

Cast off in rib.

Neatly sew cast-on edges of bands to row-end edges of collar.

See information page for finishing instructions.

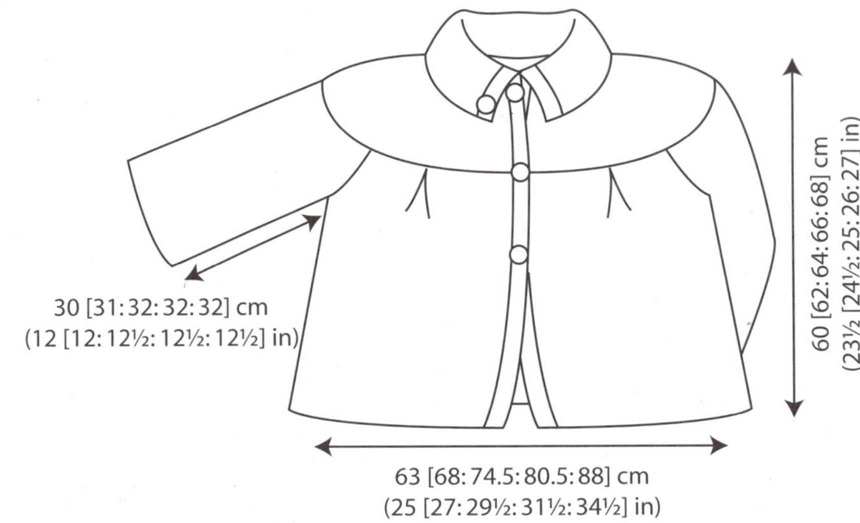

snowdrop wrap 

main image page 32

YARN

Rowan Renew

10 x 50gm

(photographed in Truck 686)

NEEDLES

1 pair 6mm (no 4) (US 10) needles

Cable needle

TENSION

24 sts and 22 rows to 10 cm measured over patt using 6mm (US 10) needles.

EXTRAS 1 x FG1067S decorative kilt pin from Bedecked. Please see credits page for contact details.

FINISHED SIZE

Completed wrap measures 120 cm (47 ins) long and 46 cm (18 ins) wide.

SPECIAL ABBREVIATIONS

C8B = slip next 4 sts onto cable needle and leave at back of work, K4, then K4 from cable needle; **C8F** = slip next 4 sts onto cable needle and leave at front of work, K4, then K4 from cable needle.

WRAP

Using 6mm (US 10) needles cast on 72 sts.

Work in g st for 6 rows, ending with RS facing for next row.

Row 7 (RS): K5, M1, (K2, M1) 31 times, K5. 104 sts.

Now work in patt as folls:

Row 1 and every foll alt row (WS): K4, P to last 4 sts, K4.

Row 2: Knit.

Row 4: K4, *C8B, rep from * to last 4 sts, K4.

Row 6: Knit.

Row 8: Knit.

Row 10: K8, *C8F, rep from * to last 8 sts, K8.

Row 12: Knit.

These 12 rows form patt.

Cont in patt until wrap meas approx 118 cm, ending after patt 1 or 7 and with RS facing for next row.

Next row (RS): K4, (K1, K2tog) 32 times, K4. 72 sts.

Work in g st for 4 rows, ending with **WS** facing for next row.

Cast off knitwise (on **WS**).

MAKING UP

Press as described on the information page.

winter cherry

main image page 12

SIZE

	S-M	L-XL	XXL	
To fit bust				
	81-97	102-117	122-127	cm
	32-38	40-46	48-50	in

YARN

Rowan Purelife British Sheep Breeds Chunky

17	18	20	x 100gm

(photographed in Mid Brown Jacob 952)

NEEDLES

1 pair 6mm (no 4) (US 10) needles
1 pair 7mm (no 2) (US 10½) needles
Cable needle

EXTRAS – 1 x FG 1067S decorative kilt pin from Bedecked. Please see credit page for contact details.

TENSION

18 sts and 22 rows to 10 cm measured over patt using 7mm (US 10½) needles.

SPECIAL ABBREVIATIONS

C4B = slip next 2 sts onto cable needle and leave at back of work, K2, then K2 from cable needle; **C4F** = slip next 2 sts onto cable needle and leave at front of work, K2, then K2 from cable needle.

BACK

Using 6mm (US 10) needles cast on 65 [83: 89] sts.
Row 1 (RS): K1, *P1, K1, rep from * to end.
Row 2: As row 1.
These 2 rows form moss st.
Work in moss st for a further 11 rows, ending with **WS** facing for next row.
Row 14 (WS): Moss st 3 [4: 5] sts, M1, (moss st 2 sts, M1, moss st 3 sts, M1) 12 [15: 16] times, moss st 2 [4: 4] sts. 90 [114: 122] sts.
Change to 7mm (UK 10½) needles.
Now work in patt as folls:
Row 1 (RS): K1, *C4B, C4F, rep from * to last st, K1.
Row 2 and every foll alt row: Purl.
Row 3: Knit.
Row 5: K1, *C4F, C4B, rep from * to last st, K1.
Row 7: Knit.
Row 8: Purl.
These 8 rows form patt.
Cont in patt until back meas 44 [46: 47] cm, ending with RS facing for next row.
Shape armholes
Keeping patt correct, cast off 4 [5: 6] sts at beg of next 2 rows. 82 [104: 110] sts.
Dec 1 st at each end of next 5 [7: 7] rows, then on foll 3 [4: 3] alt rows. 66 [82: 90] sts.
Cont straight until armhole meas 22 [24: 25] cm, ending with RS facing for next row.
Shape shoulders and back neck
Next row (RS): Cast off 9 [12: 14] sts, patt until there are 12 [16: 17] sts on right needle and turn, leaving rem sts on a holder.
Work each side of neck separately.
Cast off 3 sts at beg of next row.
Cast off rem 9 [13: 14] sts.
With RS facing, rejoin yarn to rem sts, cast off centre 24 [26: 28] sts, patt to end.
Complete to match first side, reversing shapings.

LEFT FRONT

Using 6mm (US 10) needles cast on 59 [67: 71] sts.
Work in moss st as given for back for 13 rows, ending with **WS** facing for next row.
Row 14 (WS): Moss st 10 [9: 11] sts, (moss st 2 sts, M1, moss st 3 sts, M1) 9 [11: 11] times, moss st 4 [3: 5] sts. 77 [89: 93] sts.
Change to 7mm (UK 10½) needles.
Now work in patt as folls:
Row 1 (RS): K1, *C4B, C4F, rep from * to last 12 [8: 12] sts, (C4B) 1 [0: 1] times, moss st 8 sts.
Row 2 and every foll alt row: Moss st 8 sts, P to end.
Row 3: K to last 8 sts, moss st 8 sts.
Row 5: K1, *C4F, C4B, rep from * to last 12 [8: 12] sts, (C4F) 1 [0: 1] times, moss st 8 sts.
Row 7: As row 3.
Row 8: As row 2.
These 8 rows form patt.
Cont in patt until left front matches back to beg of armhole shaping, ending with RS facing for next row.
Shape armhole
Keeping patt correct, cast off 4 [5: 6] sts at beg of next row. 73 [84: 87] sts.
Work 1 row.
Dec 1 st at armhole edge of next 5 [7: 7] rows, then on foll 3 [4: 3] alt rows. 65 [73: 77] sts.
Cont straight until left front matches back to beg of shoulder shaping, ending with RS facing for next row.
Shape shoulder
Keeping patt correct, cast off 9 [12: 14] sts at beg of next row, then 9 [13: 14] sts at beg of foll alt row. 47 [48: 49] sts.
Work 1 row, ending with RS facing for next row.
Shape hood
Keeping patt correct, cast on 16 [17: 18] sts at beg of next row. 63 [65: 67] sts.
Inc 1 st at beg of 2nd and 1 [3: 1] foll 4th rows, taking inc sts into patt. 65 [69: 69] sts.
Cont straight until hood section meas 28 cm from hood cast-on sts, ending with RS facing for next row.
Keeping patt correct, dec 1 st at beg of next and 2 foll 6th rows, then on 2 foll 4th rows, then on foll 4 alt rows, then at same edge on foll

9 rows, ending with RS facing for next row. 47 [51: 51] sts.
Cast off 5 sts at beg of next and foll 2 alt rows. 32 [36: 36] sts.
Work 1 row, ending with RS facing for next row.
Cast off.

RIGHT FRONT
Using 6mm (US 10) needles cast on 59 [67: 71] sts.
Work in moss st as given for back for 13 rows, ending with **WS** facing for next row.
Row 14 (WS): Moss st 4 [3: 5] sts, (M1, moss st 3 sts, M1, moss st 2 sts) 9 [11: 11] times, moss st 10 [9: 11] sts. 77 [89: 93] sts.
Change to 7mm (UK 10½) needles.
Now work in patt as folls:
Row 1 (RS): Moss st 8 sts, (C4F) 1 [0: 1] times, *C4B, C4F, rep from * to last st, K1.
Row 2 and every foll alt row: P to last 8 sts, moss st 8 sts.
Row 3: Moss st 8 sts, K to end.
Row 5: Moss st 8 sts, (C4B) 1 [0: 1] times, *C4F, C4B, rep from * to last st, K1.
Row 7: As row 3.
Row 8: As row 2.
These 8 rows form patt.
Complete to match left front, reversing shapings.

SLEEVES
Using 7mm (UK 10½) needles cast on 37 [39: 41] sts.
Work in moss st as given for back, shaping sides by inc 1 st at each end of 7th [5th: 5th] and every foll 8th [6th: 6th] row to 57 [43: 53] sts, then on every foll 10th [8th: 8th] row until there are 59 [63: 67] sts.
Cont straight until sleeve meas 46 [47: 47] cm, ending with RS facing for next row.
Shape top
Cast off 4 [5: 6] sts at beg of next 2 rows. 51 [53: 55] sts.
Dec 1 st at each end of next 5 rows, then on every foll alt row until 37 sts rem, then on foll 5 rows, ending with RS facing for next row. 27 sts.
Cast off 4 sts at beg of next 2 rows.
Cast off rem 19 sts.

MAKING UP
Press as described on the information page.
Join both shoulder seams using back stitch, or mattress stitch if preferred. Join top and back seam of hood section from front opening edge of final cast-off edge to cast-on sts at back neck, then sew cast-on edge of hood to back neck edge.
See information page for finishing instructions, setting in sleeves using the set-in method. Fasten fronts with decorative kilt pin as in photograph.

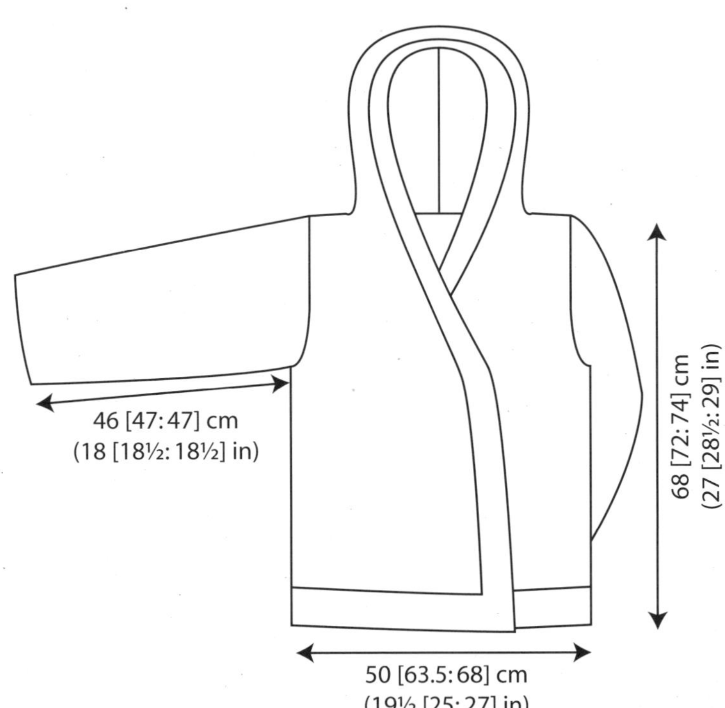

daphne

main image page 38

SIZE

S	M	L	XL	XXL	
To fit bust					
81-86	91-97	102-107	112-117	122-127	cm
32-34	36-38	40-42	44-46	48-50	in

YARN

Rowan Renew

12	13	15	16	17	x 50gm

(photographed in Garage 684)

NEEDLES

1 pair 6mm (no 4) (US 10) needles
6mm (no 4) (US 10) circular needle

TENSION

14 sts and 20 rows to 10 cm measured over st st using 6mm (US 10) needles.

LEFT BODY (knitted sideways, beg at centre back)

Using 6mm (US 10) needles cast on 113 [115: 117: 121: 123] sts.

Beg with a K row, work in st st throughout as folls:

Cont straight until work meas 25 [28: 31: 34: 37] cm, ending with RS facing for next row.

Shape sleeve

Place markers at both ends of last row to denote top of sleeve seam.

Work 4 rows, ending with RS facing for next row.

Next row (RS): K2, sl 1, K1, psso, K to last 4 sts, K2tog, K2.

Working all decreases as set by last row, dec 1 st at each end of 4th and 6 [6: 7: 5: 5] foll 4th rows, then on foll 23 [24: 23: 27: 27] alt rows. 51 [51: 53: 53: 55] sts.

Work 1 row, ending with RS facing for next row.

Next row (RS): P0 [0: 1: 1: 2], K3, *P3, K3, rep from * to last 0 [0: 1: 1: 2] sts, P0 [0: 1: 1: 2].

Next row: K0 [0: 1: 1: 2], P3, *K3, P3, rep from * to last 0 [0: 1: 1: 2] sts, K0 [0: 1: 1: 2].

Rep last 2 rows 11 times more, ending with RS facing for next row.

Cast off in rib.

RIGHT BODY (knitted sideways, beg at centre back)

With RS facing and using 6mm (US 10) needles, pick up and knit 113 [115: 117: 121: 123] sts from cast-on edge of left body – this forms centre back "seam".

Beg with a P row, work in st st throughout as folls:

Cont straight until work meas 25 [28: 31: 34: 37] cm from pick-up row, ending with RS facing for next row.

Complete as given for left body from beg of sleeve shaping.

MAKING UP

Press as described on the information page.

Join both sleeve seams from cast-off edge to marker using back stitch, or mattress stitch if preferred, reversing seam for 7 cm at cast-off edge for turn-back.

Front band

With RS facing and using 6mm (US 10) circular needle, beg and ending at base of centre back seam, pick up and knit 53 [58: 63: 70: 75] sts across row-end edge of right back to sleeve seam, 52 [57: 62: 70: 75] sts across row-end edge of right front to top of centre back seam, 52 [57: 62: 70: 75] sts across row-end edge of left front to sleeve seam, then 53 [58: 63: 70: 75] sts across row-end edge of left back to base of centre back seam. 210 [230: 250: 280: 300] sts.

Rounds 1 to 4 (RS): P1, *K3, P2, rep from * to last 4 sts, K3, P1.

Round 5: P1, *K3, P1, M1, P1, rep from * to last 4 sts, K3, P1, M1. 252 [276: 300: 336: 360] sts.

Rounds 6 to 15: P1, *K3, P3, rep from * to last 5 sts, K3, P2.

Cast off **loosely** in rib.

See information page for finishing instructions.

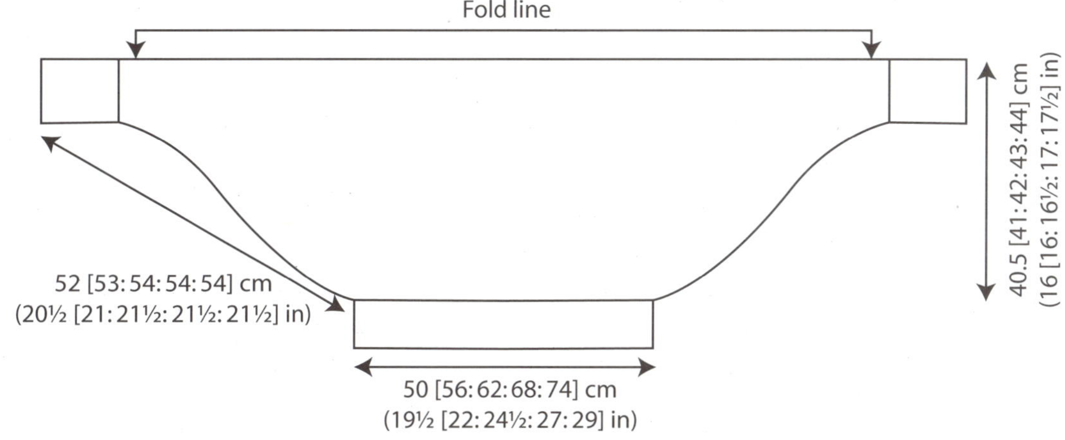

mahonia

main image page 4

SIZE

	S-M	L-XL	XXL	
To fit bust				
	81-97	102-117	122-127	cm
	32-38	40-46	48-50	in

YARN

Rowan Purelife British Sheep Breeds Chunky

11	12	13	x 100gm

(photographed in Steel Grey Suffolk 954)

NEEDLES

1 pair 6mm (no 4) (US 10) needles
1 pair 7mm (no 2) (US 10½) needles
6mm (no 4) (US 10) circular needle
Cable needle

TENSION

16½ sts and 20 rows to 10 cm measured over patt using 7mm (US 10½) needles.

SPECIAL ABBREVIATIONS

C4B = slip next 2 sts onto cable needle and leave at back of work, K2, then K2 from cable needle; **C4F** = slip next 2 sts onto cable needle and leave at front of work, K2, then K2 from cable needle; **Cr3L** = slip next 2 sts onto cable needle and leave at front of work, P1, then K2 from cable needle; **Cr3R** = slip next st onto cable needle and leave at back of work, K2, then P1 from cable needle.

BACK

Using 6mm (US 10) needles cast on 130 [150: 162] sts.
Row 1 (RS): K2, *P2, K2, rep from * to end.
Row 2: P2, *K2, P2, rep from * to end.
These 2 rows form rib.
Work in rib for a further 12 rows, dec 0 [1: 1] st at each end of last row and ending with RS facing for next row. 130 [148: 160] sts.
Change to 7mm (US 10 1/2) needles.
Now work in patt as folls:
Row 1 (RS): *P11 [14: 16], work next 16 sts as row 1 of cable panel A, P11 [14: 16]**, work next 8 sts as row 1 of cable panel B, rep from * once more, then from * to ** again.
Row 2: *K11 [14: 16], work next 16 sts as row 2 of cable panel A, K11 [14: 16]**, work next 8 sts as row 2 of cable panel B, rep from * once more, then from * to ** again.
These 2 rows set the sts – 5 cable panels with rev st st between and at sides.***
Cont as set for a further 14 [10: 22] rows, ending with RS facing for next row.
Dec row 1 (RS): *P9 [12: 14], P2tog, patt 16 sts, P2tog tbl, P9 [12: 14]**, patt 8 sts, rep from * once more, then from * to ** again. 124 [142: 154] sts.
Work 11 [9: 7] rows.
Dec row 2: *P8 [11: 13], P2tog, patt 16 sts, P2tog tbl, P8 [11: 13]**, patt 8 sts, rep from * once more, then from * to ** again. 118 [136: 148] sts.
Work 11 [9: 7] rows.
Dec row 3: *P7 [10: 12], P2tog, patt 16 sts, P2tog tbl, P7 [10: 12]**, patt 8 sts, rep from * once more, then from * to ** again. 112 [130: 142] sts.
Work 11 [9: 7] rows.
Dec row 4: *P6 [9: 11], P2tog, patt 16 sts, P2tog tbl, P6 [9: 11]**, patt 8 sts, rep from * once more, then from * to ** again. 106 [124: 136] sts.
Work 11 [9: 7] rows.
Dec row 5: *P5 [8: 10], P2tog, patt 16 sts, P2tog tbl, P5 [8: 10]**, patt 8 sts, rep from * once more, then from * to ** again. 100 [118: 130] sts.
Work 11 [9: 7] rows.
Dec row 6: *P4 [7: 9], P2tog, patt 16 sts, P2tog tbl, P4 [7: 9]**, patt 8 sts, rep from * once more, then from * to ** again. 94 [112: 124] sts.
Work 11 [9: 7] rows.
Dec row 7: *P3 [6: 8], P2tog, patt 16 sts, P2tog tbl, P3 [6: 8]**, patt 8 sts, rep from * once more, then from * to ** again. 88 [106: 118] sts.
Work 11 [9: 7] rows.
Dec row 8: *P2 [5: 7], P2tog, patt 16 sts, P2tog tbl, P2 [5: 7]**, patt 8 sts, rep from * once more, then from * to ** again. 82 [100: 112] sts.
Work 11 [9: 7] rows.
Dec row 9: *P1 [4: 6], P2tog, patt 16 sts, P2tog tbl, P1 [4: 6]**, patt 8 sts, rep from * once more, then from * to ** again. 76 [94: 106] sts.
Sizes L-XL and XXL only
Work - [9: 7] rows.
Dec row 10: *P- [3: 5], P2tog, patt 16 sts, P2tog tbl, P- [3: 5]**, patt 8 sts, rep from * once more, then from * to ** again. - [88: 100] sts.
Work - [9: 7] rows.
Dec row 11: *P- [2: 4], P2tog, patt 16 sts, P2tog tbl, P- [2: 4]**, patt 8 sts, rep from * once more, then from * to ** again. - [82: 94] sts.
Work - [9: 7] rows.
Dec row 12: *P- [1: 3], P2tog, patt 16 sts, P2tog tbl, P- [1: 3]**, patt 8 sts, rep from * once more, then from * to ** again. - [76: 88] sts.
Size XXL only
Work 7 rows.
Dec row 13: *P2, P2tog, patt 16 sts, P2tog tbl, P2**, patt 8 sts, rep from * once more, then from * to ** again. 82 sts.
Work 7 rows.
Dec row 14: *P1, P2tog, patt 16 sts, P2tog tbl, P1**, patt 8 sts, rep from * once more, then from * to ** again. 76 sts.
All sizes
Work 10 [8: 6] rows, ending with **WS** facing for next row.
Next row (WS): K2tog, patt 3 [5: 8] sts, work 2 tog, (patt 7 [10: 16] sts, work 2 tog) 7 [5: 3] times, patt 4 [5: 8] sts, K2tog. 66 [68: 70] sts.
Break yarn and leave sts on a holder.

FRONT

Work as given for back to ***.
Work a further 12 [10: 20] rows, ending with RS facing for next row.
Size L-XL only
Dec row 1 (RS): *P12, P2tog, patt 16 sts, P2tog tbl, P12**, patt 8 sts, rep from * once more,

then from * to ** again. 142 sts.
Work 7 rows, ending with RS facing for next row.

All sizes

Divide for pockets

Next row (RS): Patt 35 [39: 45] sts and turn, leaving rem sts on a holder.

Next row: Cast on and K 20 sts (for pocket back), patt to end. 55 [59: 65] sts.

Working pocket back 20 sts in rev st st as set and keeping patt correct, work 27 rows, dec 1 st at both sides of cable panel A as set by back on next and 2 [2: 3] foll 12th [10th: 8th] rows and ending with **WS** facing for next row. 49 [53: 57] sts.

Cast off 20 sts at beg of next row.

Break yarn and leave these 29 [33: 37] sts on a 2nd holder.

Return to sts left on first holder, rejoin yarn with RS facing, patt 60 [64: 70] sts and turn, leaving rem 35 [39: 45] sts on first holder.

Keeping patt correct, work 29 rows, dec 1 st at both sides of cable panel A as set by back on next and 2 [2: 3] foll 12th [10th: 8th] rows and ending with RS facing for next row. 54 [58: 62] sts.

Break yarn and leave these 54 [58: 62] sts on a 3rd holder.

Return to sts left on first holder, rejoin yarn with RS facing, cast on and P 20 sts (for pocket back), patt to end. 55 [59: 65] sts.

Working pocket back 20 sts in rev st st as set and keeping patt correct, work 28 rows, dec 1 st at both sides of cable panel A as set by back on 2nd and 2 [2: 3] foll 12th [10th: 8th] rows and ending with **WS** facing for next row. 49 [53: 57] sts.

Next row (WS): Patt 29 [33: 37] sts, cast off rem 20 sts.

Break yarn and leave these 29 [33: 37] sts on a 4th holder.

Join sections

Next row (RS): Patt across 29 [33: 37] sts on 2nd holder, then 54 [58: 62] sts on 3rd holder, then 29 [33: 37] sts on 4th holder. 112 [124: 136] sts.

Cont in patt as set across all sts, dec 1 st at both sides of each cable panel A as set by back on 8th [2nd: 4th] and 5 [7: 9] foll 12th [10th: 8th] rows. 76 sts.

Work 10 [8: 6] rows, ending with **WS** facing for next row.

Next row (WS): K2tog, patt 3 [5: 8] sts, work 2 tog, (patt 7 [10: 16] sts, work 2 tog) 7 [5: 3] times, patt 4 [5: 8] sts, K2tog. 66 [68: 70] sts.

Break yarn and leave sts on a holder.

MAKING UP

Press as described on the information page.

Mark points along each side seam edge 30 [32: 34] cm up from cast-on edge, then another point 17 cm above this point (2 markers along each side seam edge).

Side opening borders (all 4 alike)

With RS facing and using 6mm (US 10) needles, pick up and knit 23 sts evenly along row-end edge between markers.

Work in g st for 3 rows, ending with RS facing for next row.

Cast off.

Join both side seams using back stitch, or mattress stitch if preferred, leaving openings between markers and joining row-end edges of borders.

Collar

With RS facing and using 6mm (US 10) circular needle, K across 66 [68: 70] sts of front, then 66 [68: 70] sts of back. 132 [136: 140] sts.

Round 1 (RS): P1, *K2, P2, rep from * to last 3 sts, K2, P1.

Rep this round until collar meas 12 cm.

Cast off in rib.

Pocket borders (both alike)

With RS facing and using 6mm (US 10) needles, pick up and knit 28 sts evenly along row-end edge of pocket opening.

Row 1 (WS): K1, P2, *K2, P2, rep from * to last st, K1.

Row 2: K3, *P2, K2, rep from * to last st, K1.

Row 3: As row 1.

Cast off in rib.

See information page for finishing instructions.

Cable Panel A

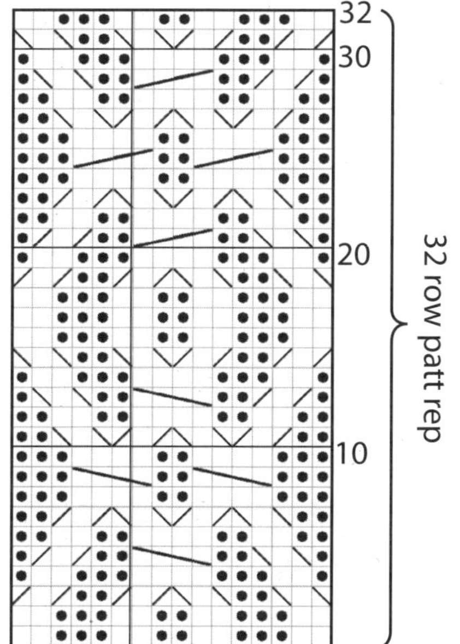

Cable Panel B

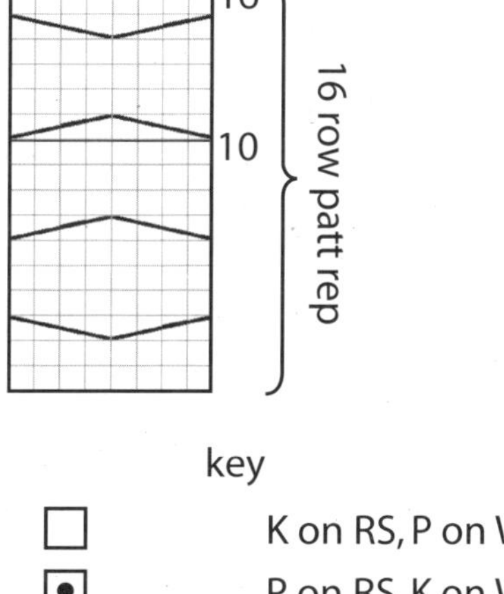

key

K on RS, P on WS

P on RS, K on WS

Cr3R

Cr3L

C4B

C4F

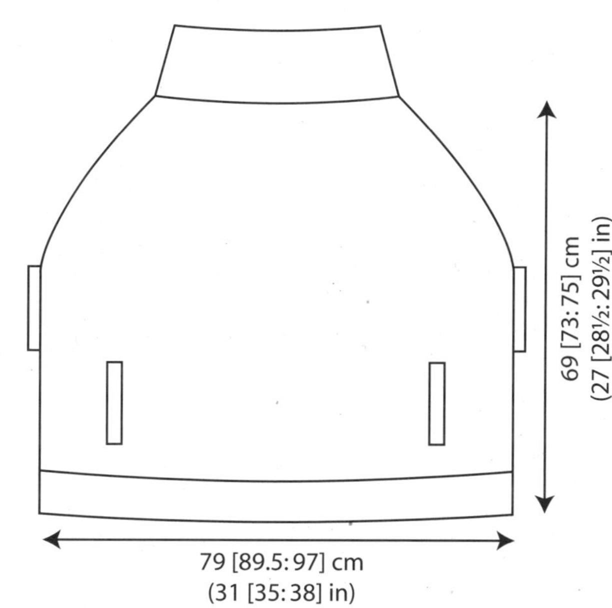

wild saffron

main image page 20

SIZE

	S-M	L-XL	XXL	
To fit bust				
	81-97	102-117	122-127	cm
	32-38	40-46	48-50	in

YARN

Rowan Renew

14	16	18	x 50gm

(photographed in Truck 686)

NEEDLES

1 pair 6mm (no 4) (US 10) needles
2 double-pointed 6mm (no 4) (US 10) needles (if required)

TENSION

21 sts and 23½ rows to 10 cm measured over patt, 14 sts and 20 rows to 10 cm measured over st st, both using 6mm (US 10) needles.

SPECIAL ABBREVIATIONS

bind 3 = sl 1 with yarn at back (WS) of work, K1, yfwd, K1, now lift the slipped st over the (K1, yfwd, K1) and off right needle; **p2sso** = pass 2 slipped sts over; **sL2togK** = slip 2 sts as though to K2tog; **wyab** = with yarn at back (RS) of work; **wyaf** = with yarn at front (RS) of work.

Pattern note: The number of sts varies whilst working patt. All st counts given relate to the **actual** number of sts on needles at that point.

BACK and FRONT (both alike)

Using 6mm (US 10) needles cast on 107 [129: 151] sts.

Work in g st for 2 rows, ending with RS facing for next row.

Beg with a K row, work in st st until work meas 24 [26: 27] cm, ending with RS facing for next row.

Now work in patt as folls:

Row 1 (RS): P2, K3, P2, *K1, sL2togK, K1, p2sso, K1, P2, K3, P2, K1, (K1, yfwd, K1) all into next st, K1, P2, K3, P2, rep from * to last 12 sts, K1, sL2togK, K1, p2sso, K1, P2, K3, P2.

Row 2: (K2, P3) twice, *K2, P3, K2, P5, K2, P3, K2, P3, rep from * to last 7 sts, K2, P3, K2.

Row 3: P2, bind 3, P2, *sl 3 wyaf, P2, bind 3, P2, K2, (K1, yfwd, K1) all into next st, K2, P2, bind 3, P2, rep from * to last 10 sts, sl 3 wyaf, P2, bind 3, P2.

Row 4: K2, P3, K2, sl 3 wyab, *K2, P3, K2, P7, K2, P3, K2, sl 3 wyab, rep from * to last 7 sts, K2, P3, K2.

Row 5: P2, K3, P2, *sl 3 wyaf, P2, K3, P2, K7, P2, K3, P2, rep from * to last 10 sts, sl 3 wyaf, P2, K3, P2.

Row 6: As row 4.

Row 7: P2, bind 3, P2, *sl 3 wyaf, P2, bind 3, P2, K2, sL2togK, K1, p2sso, K2, P2, bind 3, P2, rep from * to last 10 sts, sl 3 wyaf, P2, bind 3, P2.

Row 8: As row 2.

Row 9: P2, K3, P2, *K1, (K1, yfwd, K1) all into next st, K1, P2, K3, P2, K1, sL2togK, K1, p2sso, K1, P2, K3, P2, rep from * to last 10 sts, K1, (K1, yfwd, K1) all into next st, K1, P2, K3, P2.

Row 10: K2, P3, K2, P5, *(K2, P3) 3 times, K2, P5, rep from * to last 7 sts, K2, P3, K2.

Row 11: P2, bind 3, P2, *K2, (K1, yfwd, K1) all into next st, K2, P2, bind 3, P2, sl 3 wyaf, P2, bind 3, P2, rep from * to last 12 sts, K2, (K1, yfwd, K1) all into next st, K2, P2, bind 3, P2.

Row 12: K2, P3, K2, P7, *K2, P3, K2, sl 3 wyab, K2, P3, K2, P7, rep from * to last 7 sts, K2, P3, K2.

Row 13: P2, K3, P2, *K7, P2, K3, P2, sl 3 wyaf, P2, K3, P2, rep from * to last 14 sts, K7, P2, K3, P2.

Row 14: As row 12.

Row 15: P2, bind 3, P2, *K2, sL2togK, K1, p2sso, K2, P2, bind 3, P2, sl 3 wyaf, P2, bind 3, P2, rep from * to last 14 sts, K2, sL2togK, K1, p2sso, K2, P2, bind 3, P2.

Row 16: As row 10.

These 16 rows form patt – 4½ [5½: 6½] patt reps (plus edges sts).

Work in patt for a further 12 rows, ending with RS facing for next row.

Shape for sleeves

Taking inc sts into st st and keeping patt correct, inc 1 st at each end of next and foll 4th row, then on foll alt row, then on foll row, ending with RS facing for next row.

Changing to circular needle if required when there are too many sts to fit comfortably on needles, cont as folls:

Next row (RS): Cast on 4 sts, work across these 4 sts as folls: P1, K3, then K4, patt to last 4 sts, K4.

Next row: Cast on 4 sts, work across these 4 sts as folls: K1, P3, then P4, patt to last 8 sts, P7, K1.

Next row: Cast on 9 sts, work across these 9 sts as folls: K3, P2, K3, P1, then P1, K2, sL2togK, K1, p2sso, K2, patt to last 8 sts, K2, sL2togK, K1, p2sso, K2, P1.

Next row: Cast on 9 sts, work across these 9 sts as folls: P3, K2, P3, K1, then K1, P5, patt to last 15 sts, P5, (K2, P3) twice.

Next row: Cast on 17 sts, work across these 17 sts as folls: (P2, K3) 3 times, P2, then K1 (K1, yfwd, K1) all into next st, K1, P2, K3, P2, K1, sL2togK, K1, p2sso, K1, patt to last 15 sts, K1, sL2togK, K1, p2sso, K1, P2, K3, P2, K1, (K1, yfwd, K1) all into next st, K1.

Next row: Cast on 17 sts, work across these 17 sts as folls: (K2, P3) 3 times, K2, then P5, K2, P3, K2, P3, patt to last 32 sts, (P3, K2) twice, P5, K2, (P3, K2) 3 times.

1½ patt reps have now been increased at each side – 7½ [8½: 9½] patt reps in total (plus edges sts).

Beg with patt row 3, now work in patt across all sts as folls:

Work a further 46 [50: 54] rows, ending after patt row 4 [8: 12] (counted at centre of rows) and with RS facing for next row.

Shape shoulders and neck

Size S-M only

Next row (RS): Cast off 15 sts, patt until there are 60 sts on right needle and turn, leaving rem sts on a holder.

Work each side of neck separately.

Next row: K2tog, K1, sl 3 wyaf, patt to end.

Next row: Cast off 10 sts, patt to last 2 sts, P2tog.

Next row: P2tog, P2, K2, P3, patt to end.

Next row: Cast off 12 sts, patt to last 2 sts, K2tog.

Next row: P2tog, K2, P3, patt to end.

Next row: Cast off 12 sts, patt to last 2 sts, P2tog.

Next row: K2tog, patt to end.

Cast off rem 12 sts.

With RS facing, rejoin yarn to rem sts, cast off centre 39 sts, patt to end.

Complete to match first side, reversing shapings.

Size L-XL only

Next row (RS): Cast off 13 sts, patt until there are 68 sts on right needle and turn, leaving rem sts on a holder.

Work each side of neck separately.

Next row: K2tog, K1, P3, K2, P3, patt to end.

Next row: Cast off 12 sts, patt to last 4 sts, K3, P2tog.

Next row: P2tog, P2, K2, P3, patt to end.

Next row: Cast off 15 sts, patt to last 3 sts, K1, K2tog.

Next row: P2tog, K2, P3, K2, patt to end.

Next row: Cast off 19 sts, patt to last 3 sts, P1, P2tog.

Next row: K2tog, P3, K2, patt to end.

Cast off rem 17 sts.

With RS facing, rejoin yarn to rem sts, cast off centre 33 sts, patt to end.

Complete to match first side, reversing shapings.

Size XXL only

Next row (RS): Cast off 16 sts, patt until there are 79 sts on right needle and turn, leaving rem sts on a holder.

Work each side of neck separately.

Next row: P2tog, P4, K2, P3, patt to end.

Next row: Cast off 19 sts, patt to last 5 sts, K3, K2tog.

Next row: P2tog, P2, K2, P3, patt to end.

Next row: Cast off 17 sts, patt to last 3 sts, K1, K2tog.

Next row: P2tog, K2, P3, patt to end.

Next row: Cast off 12 sts, patt to last 3 sts, P1, P2tog.

Next row: K2tog, P3, K2, patt to end.

Cast off rem 24 sts.

With RS facing, rejoin yarn to rem sts, cast off centre 43 sts, patt to end.

Complete to match first side, reversing shapings.

MAKING UP

Press as described on the information page.

Join right shoulder seam using back stitch, or mattress stitch if preferred.

Neckband

With RS facing and using 6mm (US 10) needles, pick up and knit 8 sts down left side of front neck, 39 [33: 43] sts from front, 8 sts up right side of front neck, 8 sts down right side of back neck, 39 [33: 43] sts from back, then 8 sts up left side of back neck. 110 [98: 118] sts.

Work in g st for 2 rows, ending with **WS** facing for next row.

Cast off knitwise (on **WS**).

Join left shoulder and neckband seam.

Sleeve borders (both alike)

With RS facing and using 6mm (US 10) needles, pick up and knit 50 [56: 58] sts evenly along row-end edge of sleeve extension.

Work in g st for 2 rows, ending with **WS** facing for next row.

Cast off knitwise (on **WS**).

See information page for finishing instructions.

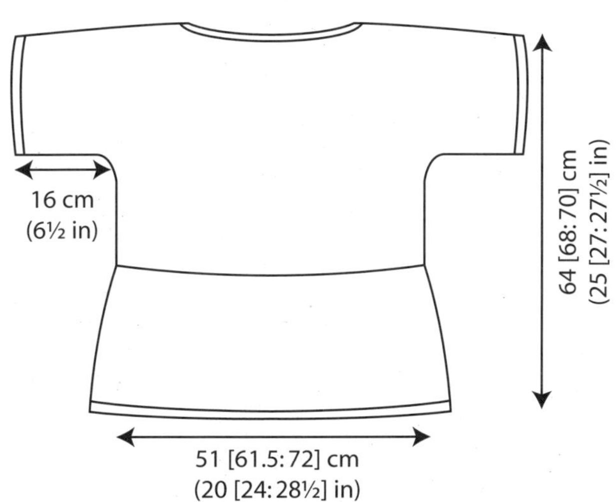

winter sweet

main image page 18

SIZE

	S	M	L	XL	XXL	
To fit bust						
	81-86	91-97	102-107	112-117	122-127	cm
	32-34	36-38	40-42	44-46	48-50	in

YARN

Rowan Renew

17	19	21	23	26	x 50gm

(photographed in Digger 682)

NEEDLES

1 pair 6mm (no 4) (US 10) needles
2 double-pointed 6mm (no 4) (US 10) needles

BUTTONS - 4 x RW5030 23mm - gunmetal, from Bedecked. Please see credits page for contact details.

TENSION

16 sts and 28 rows to 10 cm measured over g st using 6mm (US 10) needles.

BACK

Using 6mm (US 10) needles cast on 76 [84: 94: 104: 114] sts.

Beg with a RS row, work in g st throughout as folls:

Dec 1 st at each end of 23rd and 4 foll 10th rows. 66 [74: 84: 94: 104] sts.

Work 13 rows, ending with RS facing for next row.

Inc 1 st at each end of next and foll 16th row. 70 [78: 88: 98: 108] sts.

Cont straight until back meas 42 [43: 44: 45: 46] cm, ending with RS facing for next row.

Shape raglan armholes

Cast off 3 sts at beg of next 2 rows. 64 [72: 82: 92: 102] sts.

Dec 1 st at each end of next 1 [1: 1: 1: 5] rows, then on 9 [6: 4: 0: 0] foll 4th rows, then on foll 8 [15: 21: 30: 30] alt rows, then on foll row, ending with RS facing for next row. 26 [26: 28: 28: 30] sts.

Cast off **very firmly.**

POCKET LININGS (make 2)

Using 6mm (US 10) needles cast on 24 sts.

Beg with a RS row, work in g st for 41 rows, ending with **WS** facing for next row.

Break yarn and leave sts on a holder.

LEFT FRONT

Using 6mm (US 10) needles cast on 42 [46: 51: 56: 61] sts.

Beg with a RS row, work in g st throughout as folls:

Dec 1 st at beg of 23rd and 2 foll 10th rows. 39 [43: 48: 53: 58] sts.

Work 6 rows, ending with **WS** facing for next row.

Place pocket

Next row (WS): K11 [14: 17: 20: 24], cast off next 24 sts knitwise, K to end.

Next row: K4 [5: 7: 9: 10], with RS facing K across 24 sts of first pocket lining, K to end. 39 [43: 48: 53: 58] sts.

Dec 1 st at beg of 2nd and foll 10th row. 37 [41: 46: 51: 56] sts.

Work 13 rows, ending with RS facing for next row.

Inc 1 st at beg of next and foll 16th row. 39 [43: 48: 53: 58] sts.

Cont straight until left front matches back to beg of raglan armhole shaping, ending with RS facing for next row.

Shape raglan armhole

Cast off 3 sts at beg of next row. 36 [40: 45: 50: 55] sts.

Work 1 row.

Dec 1 st at raglan armhole edge of next 1 [1: 1: 1: 5] rows, then on 3 [3: 3: 0: 0] foll 4th rows, then on foll 0 [0: 0: 6: 4] alt rows. 32 [36: 41: 43: 46] sts.

Work 1 row, ending with RS facing for next row.

Shape front slope

Dec 1 st at raglan armhole edge of 3rd [3rd: 3rd: next: next] and 5 [2: 0: 0: 0] foll 4th rows, then on foll 5 [12: 18: 20: 22] alt rows **and at same time** dec 1 st at end of next 5 [3: 1: 1: 1] rows, then on foll 14 [16: 19: 19: 19] alt rows, then on 0 [0: 0: 0: 1] foll 4th row. 2 sts.

Work 1 row, ending with RS facing for next row.

Next row (RS): K2tog and fasten off.

Mark positions for 4 buttons along left front opening edge – first to come in row 17, last to come just below beg of front slope shaping and rem 2 buttons evenly spaced between.

RIGHT FRONT

Using 6mm (US 10) needles cast on 42 [46: 51: 56: 61] sts.

Beg with a RS row, work in g st throughout as folls:

Work 16 rows, ending with RS facing for next row.

Next row (buttonhole row) (RS): K3, cast off 2 sts (to make a buttonhole – cast on 2 sts over these cast-off sts on next row), K to end.

Making a further 3 buttonholes in this way to correspond with positions marked for buttons and noting that no further reference will be made to buttonholes, cont as folls:

Dec 1 st at end of 6th and 2 foll 10th rows. 39 [43: 48: 53: 58] sts.

Work 6 rows, ending with **WS** facing for next row.

Place pocket

Next row (WS): K4 [5: 7: 9: 10], cast off next

24 sts knitwise, K to end.
Next row: K11 [14: 17: 20: 24], with RS facing K across 24 sts of second pocket lining, K to end. 39 [43: 48: 53: 58] sts.
Dec 1 st at end of 2nd and foll 10th row. 37 [41: 46: 51: 56] sts.
Complete to match left front, reversing shapings.

SLEEVES
Using 6mm (US 10) needles cast on 36 [36: 38: 38: 40] sts.
Beg with a RS row, work in g st, shaping sides by inc 1 st at each end of 7th [7th: 7th: 7th: 5th] and every foll 8th [8th: 8th: 8th: 6th] row to 42 [48: 58: 68: 48] sts, then on every foll 10th [10th: 10th: -: 8th] row until there are 60 [62: 66: -: 72] sts.
Cont straight until sleeve meas 46 [47: 48: 48: 48] cm, ending with RS facing for next row.
Shape raglan
Cast off 3 sts at beg of next 2 rows. 54 [56: 60: 62: 66] sts.
Dec 1 st at each end of next and 3 foll 4th rows, then on every foll alt row until 12 sts rem.
Work 1 row, ending with RS facing for next row.
Left sleeve only
Dec 1 st at each end of next row, then cast off 2 sts at beg of foll row. 8 sts.
Dec 1 st at each end of next row, then dec 1 st at beg of foll row. 5 sts.
Right sleeve only
Cast off 2 sts at beg and dec 1 st at end of next row, then dec 1 st at end of foll row. 8 sts.
Dec 1 st at each end of next row, then dec 1 st at end of foll row. 5 sts.
Both sleeves
Rep last 2 rows once more.
Next row (RS): K2tog and fasten off.

MAKING UP
Press as described on the information page.
Join all raglan seams using back stitch, or mattress stitch if preferred.
Collar
With RS facing and using 6mm (US 10) needles, beg and ending at beg of front slope shaping, pick up and knit 34 [36: 40: 42: 46] sts up right front slope, 8 sts from top of right sleeve, 28 [28: 30: 30: 32] sts from back, 8 sts from top of left sleeve, then 34 [36: 40: 42: 46] sts down left front slope. 112 [116: 126: 130: 140] sts.
Row 1 (RS of collar, WS of body): K17 [15: 16: 14: 15], inc in next st, *K3, inc in next st, rep from * to last 18 [16: 17: 15: 16] sts, K to end. 132 [138: 150: 156: 168] sts.
Row 2: K84 [87: 94: 97: 104], wrap next st (by slipping next st on left needle onto right needle, taking yarn to opposite side of work between needles and then slipping same st back onto left needle – when working back across wrapped sts, work the wrapped st and the wrapping loop tog as one st) and turn.
Row 3: K36 [36: 38: 38: 40], wrap next st and turn.
Row 4: K39 [39: 41: 41: 43], wrap next st and turn.
Row 5: K42 [42: 44: 44: 46], wrap next st and turn.
Row 6: K45 [45: 47: 47: 49], wrap next st and turn.
Row 7: K48 [48: 50: 50: 52], wrap next st and turn.
Row 8: K51 [51: 53: 53: 55], wrap next st and turn.
Row 9: K54 [54: 56: 56: 58], wrap next st and turn.
Cont in this way, working 3 more sts on every row before wrapping next st and turning, until the foll row has been worked:
Next row (RS of collar): K126 [132: 146: 152: 160], wrap next st and turn.
Next row: K to end.
Next row: Knit.
Cast off all sts **loosely** knitwise (on **WS** of collar).
Front and neck trim
Using double-pointed 6mm (US 10) needles cast on 3 sts.
Row 1 (RS): K3, *without turning slip these 3 sts to opposite end of needle and bring yarn to opposite end of work pulling it quite tightly across **WS** of work, K these 3 sts again, rep from * until trim, when very slightly stretched and beg and ending at cast-on edges, fits up right front opening edge, along cast-off edge of collar, then down left front opening edge.
Cast off.
Neatly slip stitch trim in place.
Pocket trims (both alike)
Work as given for front and neck trim, making a strip that fits neatly across cast-off edge of pocket opening.
Neatly slip stitch trims in place.
See information page for finishing instructions.

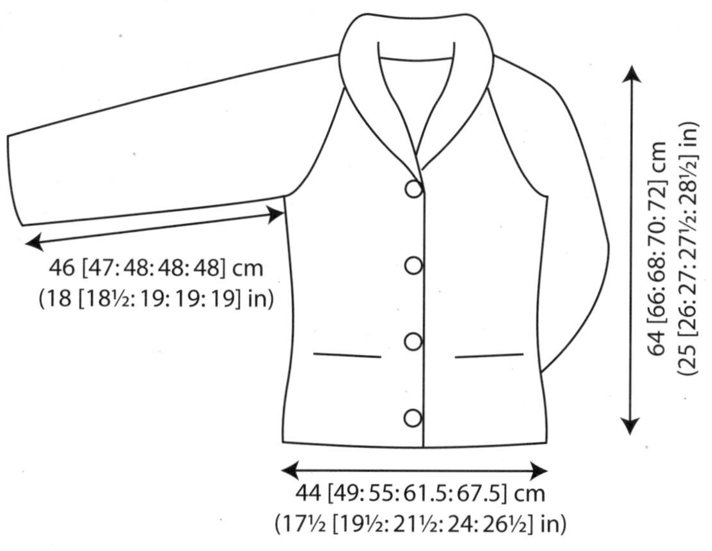

information page

Tension
Obtaining the correct tension is perhaps the single factor which can make the difference between a successful garment and a disastrous one. It controls both the shape and size of an article, so any variation, however slight, can distort the finished garment. Different designers feature in our books and it is their tension, given at the start of each pattern, which you must match. We recommend that you knit a square in pattern and/or stocking stitch (depending on the pattern instructions) of perhaps 5 – 10 more stitches and 5 – 10 more rows than those given in the tension note. Mark out the central 10cm square with pins. If you have too many stitches to 10cm try again using thicker needles, if you have too few stitches to 10cm try again using finer needles. Once you have achieved the correct tension your garment will be knitted to the measurements indicated in the size diagram shown at the end of the pattern.

Sizing and Size Diagram Note
The instructions are given for the smallest size.Where they vary, work the figures in brackets for the larger sizes. **One set of figures refers to all sizes.** Included with most patterns in this brochure is a **"size diagram"**, of the finished garment and its dimensions. The measurement shown at the bottom of each **"size diagram"** shows the garment width 2.5cm below the armhole shaping. To help you choose the size of garment to knit please refer to the new sizing guide.

Chart Note
Many of the patterns in the book are worked from charts. Each square on a chart represents a stitch and each line of squares a row of knitting. Each colour used is given a different letter and these are shown in the materials section, or in the key alongside the chart of each pattern.
When working from the charts, read odd rows (K) from right to left and even rows (P) from left to right, unless otherwise stated.

Finishing Instructions
After working for hours knitting a garment, it seems a great pity that many garments are spoiled because such little care is taken in the pressing and finishing process. Follow the following tips for a truly professional looking garment.

Pressing
Block out each piece of knitting and following the instructions on the ball band press the garment pieces, omitting the ribs.

Tip
Take special care to press the edges, as this will make sewing up both easier and neater. If the ball band indicates that the fabric is not to be pressed, then covering the blocked out fabric with a damp white cotton cloth and leaving it to stand will have the desired effect. Darn in all ends neatly along the selvage edge or a colour join, as appropriate.

Stitching
When stitching the pieces together, remember to match areas of colour and texture very carefully where they meet. Use a seam stitch such as back stitch or mattress stitch for all main
knitting seams and join all ribs and neckband with mattress stitch, unless otherwise stated.

Construction
Having completed the pattern instructions, join left shoulder and neckband seams as detailed above. Sew the top of the sleeve to the body of the garment using the method detailed in the pattern, referring to the appropriate guide:

Straight cast-off sleeves
Place centre of cast-off edge of sleeve to shoulder seam. Sew top of sleeve to body, using markers as guidelines where applicable.

Square set-in sleeves
Place centre of cast-off edge of sleeve to shoulder seam. Set sleeve head into armhole, the straight sides at top of sleeve to form a neat rightangle to cast-off sts at armhole on back and front.

Shallow set-in sleeves
Place centre of cast off edge of sleeve to shoulder seam. Match decreases at beg of armhole shaping to decreases at top of sleeve. Sew sleeve head into armhole, easing in shapings.

Set-in sleeves
Place centre of cast-off edge of sleeve to shoulder seam. Set in sleeve, easing sleeve head into armhole.

Join side and sleeve seams.
Slip stitch pocket edgings and linings into place.
Sew on buttons to correspond with buttonholes.
Ribbed welts and neckbands and any areas of garter stitch should not be pressed.

abbreviations

K	knit
P	purl
st(s)	stitch(es)
inc	increas(e)(ing)
dec	decreas(e)(ing)
st st	stocking stitch (1 row K, 1 row P)
g st	garter stitch (K every row)
beg	begin(ning)
foll	following
rem	remain(ing)
rev st st	reverse stocking stitch (1 row K, 1row P)
rep	repeat
alt	alternate
cont	continue
patt	pattern
tog	together
mm	millimetres
cm	centimetres
in(s)	inch(es)
RS	right side
WS	wrong side
sl 1	slip one stitch
psso	pass slipped stitch over
p2sso	pass 2 slipped stitches over
tbl	through back of loop
M1	make one stitch by picking up horizontal loop before next stitch and knitting into back of it
M1P	make one stitch by picking up horizontal loop before next stitch and purling into back of it
yfwd	yarn forward
yrn	yarn round needle
meas	measures
0	no stitches, times or rows
-	no stitches, times or rows for that size
yon	yarn over needle
yfrn	yarn forward round needle
wyib	with yarn at back

experience ratings

Easy, straight forward knitting

Suitable for the average knitter

Suitable for the more experienced knitter

Our sizing now conforms to standard clothing sizes. Therefore if you buy a standard size 12 in clothing, then our size 12 or medium patterns will fit you perfectly. Dimensions in the charts shown are body measurements, not garment dimensions, therefore please refer to the measuring guide to help you to determine which is the best size for you to knit.

CASUAL SIZING GUIDE FOR WOMEN

As there are some designs that are intended to fit more generously, we have introduced our casual sizing guide. The designs that fall into this group can be recognised by the size range: Small, Medium, Large & Xlarge. Each of these sizes cover two sizes from the standard sizing guide, ie. Size S will fit sizes 8/10, size M will fit sizes 12/14 and so on. The sizing within this chart is also based on the larger size within the range, ie. M will be based on size 14.

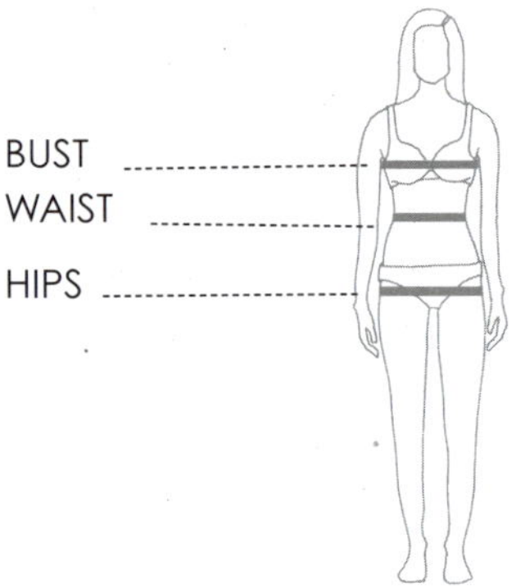

UK SIZE DUAL SIZE	S 8/10	M 12/14	L 16/18	XL 20/22	XXL 24/26	
To fit bust	32 - 34	36 - 38	40 - 42	44 - 46	48 - 50	inches
	81 - 86	91 - 97	102 - 107	112 - 117	122 - 127	cm
To fit waist	24 - 26	28 - 30	32 - 34	36 - 38	40 - 42	inches
	61 - 66	71 - 76	81 - 86	91 - 97	102 - 107	cm
To fit hips	34 - 36	38 - 40	42 - 44	46 - 48	50 - 52	inches
	86 - 91	97 - 102	107 - 112	117 - 122	127 - 132	cm

MEASURING GUIDE

For maximum comfort and to ensure the correct fit when choosing a size to knit, please follow the tips below when checking your size.
Measure yourself close to your body, over your underwear and don't pull the tape measure too tight!
Bust/chest – measure around the fullest part of the bust/chest and across the shoulder blades.
Waist – measure around the natural waistline, just above the hip bone.
Hips – measure around the fullest part of the bottom.
If you don't wish to measure yourself, note the size of a favourite jumper that you like the fit of. Our sizes are now comparable to the clothing sizes from the major high street retailers, so if your favourite jumper is a size Medium or size 12, then our casual size Medium and standard size 12 should be approximately the same fit.
To be extra sure, measure your favourite jumper and then compare these measurements with the Rowan size diagram given at the end of the individual instructions.
Finally, once you have decided which size is best for you, please ensure that you achieve the tension required for the design you wish to knit.
Remember if your tension is too loose, your garment will be bigger than the pattern size and you may use more yarn. If your tension is too tight, your garment could be smaller than the pattern size and you will have yarn left over.
Furthermore if your tension is incorrect, the handle of your fabric will be too stiff or floppy and will not fit properly. It really does make sense to check your tension before starting every project.

stockists

AUSTRALIA: Australian Country Spinners Pty Ltd, Level 7, 409 St. Kilda Road, Melbourne 3004. Tel: 03 9380 3830 Email: tkohut@auspinners.com.au

AUSTRIA: Coats Harlander GmbH, Autokaderstrasse 31, Wien A -1210. Tel: (01) 27716

BELGIUM: Coats Benelux, Ring Oost 14A, Ninove, 9400 Tel: 054 318989 Email: sales.coatsninove@coats.com

CANADA: Westminster Fibers, 8 Shelter Drive, Greer, South Carolina, 29650 Tel: 800 445-9276 Email: info@westminsterfibers.com Web: www.westminsterfibers.com

CHINA: Coats Shanghai Ltd, No 9 Building , Baosheng Road, Songjiang Industrial Zone, Shanghai. Tel: 86 21 5774 3733 Email: victor.li@coats.com

DENMARK: Coats HP A/S, Tagensvej 85C, St.tv., Copenhagen Tel: 45 35 86 90 49

FINLAND: Coats Opti Crafts Oy, Ketjutie 3, Kerava , 04220 Tel: (358) 9 274871 Email: coatsopti@coats.com Web: wwwcoatscrafts.fi

FRANCE: Coats Steiner, 100 Avenue du Général de Gaulle, Mehun-Sur-Yèvre, 18500 Tel: 02 48 23 12 30 Web: www.coatscrafts.fr

GERMANY: Coats GmbH, Kaiserstrasse 1, Kenzingen, 79341 Tel: 07162-14346 Web: www.coatsgmbh.de

HOLLAND: Coats Benelux, Ring Oost 14A, Ninove, 9400, Belgium Tel: 0346 35 37 00 Email: sales.coatsninove@coats.com

HONG KONG: Coats Shanghai Ltd, No 8 Building , Export & Processing Garden, Songjiang Industrial Zone, Shanghai, China. Tel: (86- 21) 57743733-326 Email: victor.li@coats.com

ICELAND: Rowan At Storkurinn, Laugavegur 59, Reykjavik, 101 Tel: 551 8258 Email: storkurinn@simnet.is Web: www.storkurinn.is

ISRAEL: Beit Hasidkit, Ms. Offra Tzenger, Sokolov St No 2, Kfar Sava, 44256 Tel: (972) 9 7482381

ITALY: Coats cucirini srl, Viale sarca no 223, Milano, 20126

KOREA: Coats Korea Co. Lt, 5F Eyeon B/D, 935-40 Bangbae-Dong, Seocho-Gu, Seoul, 137-060 Tel: 82-2-521-6262 Web: www.coatskorea.co.kr

LEBANON: y.knot, Saifi Village, Mkhalissiya Street 162, Beirut Tel: (961) 1 992211 Email: y.knot@cyberia.net.lb

LUXEMBOURG: Coats Benelux, Ring Oost 14A, Ninove, 9400, Belgium Tel: 0346 35 37 00 Email: sales.coatsninove@coats.com

MALTA: John Gregory Ltd, 8 Ta'Xbiex Sea Front, Msida, MSD 1512, Malta Tel: +356 2133 0202 Email: raygreg@onvol.net

NEW ZEALAND: ACS New Zealand, 1 March Place, Belfast, Christchurch Tel: 64-3-323-6665

NORWAY: Coats Knappehuset AS, Pb 100, Ulset, Bergen, 5873 Tel: 55 53 93 00

PORTUGAL: Coats & Clark, Quinta de Cravel, Apartado 444, Vila Nova de Gaia 4431-968 Tel: 223770700 Web: www.crafts.com.pt

SINGAPORE: Golden Dragon Store, 101 Upper Cross Street, #02-51, People's Park Centre, 058357, Singapore Tel: (65) 65358454/65358234 Email: gdscraft@hotmail.com

SOUTH AFRICA: Arthur Bales Ltd, 62 Fourth Avenue, Linden, Johannesburg, 2195 Tel: (27) 118 882 401 Email: arthurb@new.co.za Web: www.arthurbales.co.za

SPAIN: Coats Fabra, SA, Santa Adria, 20, Barcelona, 08030 Tel: (34) 93 290 84 00 Email: atencion.clientes@coats.com Web: www.coatscrafts.es

SWEDEN: Coats Expotex AB, JA Wettergrensgata 7, Vastra Frolunda, Goteborg, 431 30 Tel: (46) 33 720 79 00

SWITZERLAND: Coats Stroppel AG, Turgi (AG), CH-5300 Tel: 056 298 12 20

TAIWAN: Cactus Quality Co Ltd, 7FL-2, No. 140, Sec. 2 Roosevelt Road, Taipei, Taiwan, R.O.C. 10084 Tel: 00886-2-23656527 Email:cqcl@ms17.hinet.net Web: www.excelcraft.com.tw

THAILAND: Global Wide Trading, 10 Lad Prao Soi 88, Bangkok 10310 Tel: 00 662 933 9019 Email: TheNeedleWorld@yahoo.com – global.wide@yahoo.com

U.S.A.: Westminster Fibers Inc, 8 Shelter Drive, Greer, 29650, South Carolina Tel: (800) 445-9276 Email: info@westminsterfibers.com Web: www.westminsterfibers.com

U.K: Rowan, Green Lane Mill, Holmfirth, West Yorkshire, England HD9 2DX Tel: +44 (0) 1484 681881 Email: mail@knitrowan.com Web: www.knitrowan.com

For stockists in all other countries please contact Rowan for details

notes

notes

Photographer • Kristin Perers
Art Direction & Sylist • Rowan
Hair & Make-up • Frances Prescott (One Photographic)
Models • George (Select Model Managment)
Design Layout • Rowan
Location • Many thanks to Arnie & William of Allt-Y-Bela, Llangwm, Ucha, Usk, Monmothshire

Handknitters • Judith Chamberlain, Audrey Kidd, Sandra Taylor, Wendy Shipman, Lorrainne Heam, Margaret Morris, Elizabeth Jones, Honey Ingram, Teressa Gogay, Sandra Richardson, Maisie Laing, Janet Oakey, Elisie Eland, Jane Duffy, Andrea McHugh, Fiona McCabe, Cynthia Noble, Paula Dukes

Buttons • Bedecked Ltd, 1 Castle Wall, Back Fold, Hay-On-Wye, Via Hereford, HR3 5EQ
shop tel: 01497 822769
web: www.bedecked.co.uk
email: thegirls@bedecked.co.uk

First published in Great Britain in 2010 by Rowan Yarns Ltd, Green Lane Mill, Holmfirth, West Yorkshire, England, HD9 2DX
Internet: www.knitrowan.com

British Library Cataloguing in Publication Data Rowan Yarns - Purelife Autumn
ISBN 978-1-906007-84-3